KAYLA WREN

After Class

BLACK CHERRY
PUBLISHING

First edition

ISBN: 978-1-914242-37-3

This book was professionally typeset on Reedsy.
Find out more at reedsy.com

Contents

Keep in touch with Kayla!

Want to hear about new releases, sales, bonus content and other cool stuff? Sign up for Kayla's newsletter at www.kaylawrenauthor.com/newsletter!

1

Chapter One

"Wouldn't it be hilarious if Raine and Fraser got together?"

Lucy and Keeley chatter loudly as we walk through the rain-slicked city streets, hopping over puddles that glow orange with lamplight. I trail behind, hands in my jacket pockets, no hint of emotion on my face.

Gideon and Beckett laugh too, walking two steps behind me, but more nervously than the girls. The two ex-professors are both devoted to their girlfriends, but there's no denying they gave up a lot for them. Neither of them teach any more, with Gideon working as a writer and critic and Beckett working hours away up the coast to coach an elite rowing team. He drives back down every weekend to spend time with Keeley, and spends most weeknights talking to her on the phone.

No one could blame them for not wanting that for their friend.

To an outsider, they lost out. Gave up esteemed careers as professors to quickly sidestep into other jobs. And the rumors swirled behind them on campus—baseless rumors about sleeping with tons of students and abusing their power.

None of those are true. Obviously. Any idiot can look at these two men and see they fell in love. Gideon is hypnotized by Lucy, staring at her walking ahead of him like he still can't believe she's real. And Beckett is almost painfully tender with Keeley, treasuring her like she's the center of his universe.

I guess I wouldn't mind some of that. Someone worshipping the ground I walk on. I'm only human.

But something tells me it won't come from some dusty old professor. In all honesty, I'm not even sure I'm capable of those things anyway.

Attraction.

Desire.

Feeling such strong emotions for someone that I can't keep away—and inspiring those same feelings in someone else.

Let's just say that I've had a very peaceful college experience so far. I've tried hook-ups, sure. As a personal experiment more than anything. And they were okay, but not worth the awkwardness. And though I've heard plenty about this Fraser—even looked up his staff profile online—I can't picture it.

He seems stuffy. Boring. Cold.

Nothing like the man I'd need to bring me to life. To wake up all the latent feelings and desires that I'm only half-sure are in there somewhere. A big part of me wonders whether it's even real for anyone else, or if they're all exaggerating too to fit in.

But then Beckett comes to visit, and Keeley's walls are thin. So I know it's real.

I suppose tonight is an experiment of sorts. I hop over a puddle, cheered by the thought. It's spring in the city, which means wet and breezy weather with flashes of pale sunshine in the day. And in the nights like these, it might as well still be winter. I burrow my chin into my jacket collar and tune out the girls' chatter. We're meeting for drinks to celebrate Gideon's book deal, but I know Lucy and Keeley are both hoping the last professor and I will feel a spark.

Fraser Drummond is a psychology professor. One of the big names in my department. But he's never taught me—he's on some weird sabbatical as a guidance counselor—so I've never really seen him up close.

I seriously doubt he can solve my attraction problem. But maybe he can give some academic answers. Point me towards some helpful research papers or something.

Maybe Fraser Drummond can set me a private assignment.

* * *

Professor Fraser Drummond is... kind of rude.

Not outright. He doesn't say anything brash or insulting; he doesn't sneer or roll his eyes. But when we slide one by one into the booth at the bar, and our eyes meet across the table, he nods once and looks away. He turns to the conversation happening between Keeley and Gideon, her bright stream of questions about his book, and I can practically see Fraser tuning me out. Putting up invisible walls.

Dismissed. Just like that.

I haven't even asked him yet about the psychology of attraction.

I peer at him with narrowed eyes, examining him openly across the booth table. The professor has thick coppery hair and piercing blue eyes, and pale, clean-shaven skin. He's so pale, he looks ghostly. If my mother saw him, she'd chase him outside and tell him to get some sun. At first glance, he seems slender, but only because he's sat next to Beckett. When I look at him, really look, I realize his shoulders are broad. Toned.

I scowl down at my whisky and take a sip. He glances over, his eyes ghosting over my drink before he looks away.

Nothing. Not a flicker of emotion or reaction. This man is infuriating.

The whisky spreads over my tongue, smoky and delicious, and I lick a bead of moisture off my top lip. The slightest frown creases his forehead, but he stays fixated on Gideon, grip tight on his beer bottle.

Fine. Whatever. I don't want to talk to a rude asshole anyway.

"Fraser, how's the study going?"

Apparently Lucy knows him well enough. I perk up, straining to hear his low voice over the din of the bar.

He shrugs and offers her a small smile. "I've paused my research activities."

I sink back against the seat, disappointed. If I were a psychology professor, you'd better believe I'd be heading up studies. Starting projects and focus groups; researching the mysteries of the human brain.

This guy doesn't know how lucky he is.

"Raine's a psychology major." Lucy nods at me, a wicked glint in her eye. "You two should have loads to talk about."

The professor glances at me, his eyes sliding away as quickly as they came. Another shrug.

Asshole.

"I don't teach any more."

"Why not?" I blurt out. He looks at me again, the movement sharp. I glare back. This grumpy ghost of a man doesn't intimidate me.

4

He opens his mouth to answer, but then closes it again. Something stirs deep in his eyes, something troubled and panicked, but then Beckett swoops to his rescue.

"Fraser's a do-gooder." He claps his friend on the shoulder. "He's too busy saving troubled souls as a guidance counselor."

That's not it, I want to scream, but apparently no one else can see it—the haunted look in this man's eyes. They all nod and smile and talk about how good he is, how giving, and can't they see that they're making it worse? His face drains impossibly paler, almost gray, and he swallows hard as he forces a smile.

When his gaze lands on me again, he jerks back slightly. I'm scowling at him, trying to unpick his secrets. If I could, I'd reach over and tilt his head to the side, cupping my hand beneath his ear as those glittering secrets dropped into my palm.

His eyes narrow, his expression darkening, those icy eyes still fixed on mine, and something coils in my abdomen. Something hot and aching.

Oh.

I press my thighs together, shifting on my seat, never breaking the eye contact between us. Somehow he reads that motion too, something knowing and almost cruel in the way he watches me, and my skin flushes to a thousand degrees.

I want to catalogue these sensations. Make a bullet pointed list so that I can compare them to the academic notes on attraction on my laptop. There's the hollow, aching feeling in my core, twisting tighter with every breath, and the way my pulse thrums faster under my skin. Colors are brighter; every sound and smell is heightened, and god, what does this man smell like?

I swipe my whisky glass off the table with a trembling hand. It burns the back of my throat, anchoring me back to reality.

When I place the glass back down with a thud, he finally, finally, looks away.

My breath leaves my chest. I wilt back against the leather seats.

I feel like I've just done one of Keeley's horrible work outs.

This is it. This is perfect! I sit up ramrod straight, my mind racing as I tune out the conversation. Sure, he's rude and standoffish, clearly damaged in some way, but that's not the point. Professor Fraser Drummond makes me *feel*.

Surely he won't refuse to help me explore these sensations. Even just academically.

You know. For science.

2

Chapter Two

I lean back in my office chair and rub my hands along the armrests. The young man in front of me mumbles, tripping over his words as he tries to explain how lost he feels. His eyes dart to me then back to his knees, his fingers twisting in his lap, and every time he meets my eyes I give an encouraging nod.

I don't laugh. I don't make light of his problems. I don't pull any of the easy escape tactics that his friends do. I sit here and listen to him, every single word, and I take him seriously.

This is my job since I stopped teaching. This is what I do.

Sometimes, the students build themselves up for weeks to come here, to make an appointment, but when they finally sit across from me, they have no words. Not for their real issues. I listen to those students too, even when they chatter about everything except what's really bothering them. I nod and ask questions about their classes and their friends and their homesickness, all in the hope that next time, we'll get a bit further.

It's respectable work. Worthwhile. I'm helping people, adding crumbs of good to the world, and so far no one has noticed that it's all a sham.

Oh, the advice is real. And I do care about these students, in the distant way you care for strangers.

But it's not me. It's not what I intended for myself when I flew across an ocean to come here. And in the shadowy, shameful depths of my soul… I'm bored.

As lost and unchallenged as the young man sitting across from me.

"Do you have coping mechanisms?" I ask when he stutters to a halt. His brow wrinkles in confusion, so I elaborate. "Things you can do which help you to feel better. When the anxiety becomes overwhelming."

The student pauses. His fingers twist in his lap, tighter and tighter, the knuckles turning white.

"Um." His voice is rough. "Drinking?"

I shake my head, mouth twitching.

"That's not advised."

He grins at me, relieved that we can joke about this. That I won't lecture him or report him or whatever else the students worry about when they come to me.

"Try again," I prompt. "What things do you do automatically when you've had a rough day?"

He shrugs one shoulder. "I, uh. Write in a journal, I guess?" His cheeks flush, like that's somehow weak or feminine or something to be ashamed of.

"Excellent." I nod and sit forward, propping my elbows on my knees, and the student smiles again, relieved. "That's a well known and popular coping mechanism. You've done well to discover it on your own."

He sits straighter. Nods to himself, rubbing his palms along his jeans. I'm not a psychiatrist or a therapist—I'm not here to diagnose illness or prescribe treatment. But it's still good to see the students leave lighter than when they came in.

This is something I can do, at least. For them, if not for myself.

The student leaves on the hour, shouldering his backpack and giving an awkward wave before he lets himself out. As soon as the door snaps shut, I push to my feet, my limbs buzzing with nervous energy. My office is small but rectangular, and I pace up and down the short length of it, scrubbing a hand at the back of my neck.

I should be happy.

Or content, at least.

I have everything I need: a steady paycheck, a warm apartment, good friends here and loving family back in Scotland. There's even a promising academic career waiting for me just as soon as I stop running away from it. And there's a damn trust fund with my name on it, if I only weren't so proud.

I groan, raking a hand through my hair. If only I could run away from my own bullshit, but alas, I seem to follow myself everywhere.

The knock on the door makes me jerk. I glance at the clock on the wall, wracking my brain for a forgotten appointment, but I draw a blank. There's no one scheduled.

A drop-in, then. I blow out a breath. These are often the hardest; the most desperate souls. I cross to my desk and sink into the chair, willing my racing heart to calm down.

Coping mechanisms. I could use a few of my own.

A second knock sounds, and I clear my throat, heart sinking. "Come in."

* * *

I recognize this girl. The door opens a crack, her head poking through the gap, and awareness tickles my gut. It takes a second for me to place her—her smooth brown skin, her large, dark eyes, the piercing winking from the side of her nose—but when I do, alarm bells sound in the back of my head.

It's Lucy and Keeley's friend. The girl from the bar. The one who scowled at me like a Persian cat, who watched me with coolness and unrestrained hunger at the same time.

Raine.

Shit.

I open my mouth to tell her I'll find her another guidance counselor. One who doesn't know her socially—one she hasn't looked at like they're something to eat. But she's already come in and closed the door with a snap, marching across my tiny office and throwing herself into the chair opposite mine.

"Ah." I clear my throat. "Hello, Raine."

She beams at me. "You remembered! Good. That will make this easier."

Those alarm bells sound louder, deafening my brain, but she shuffles around on the seat trying to get comfortable.

"This is horrible." She quirks an eyebrow. "Do you make the students uncomfortable on purpose? Is it a tactic?"

"This is the Student Wellness Center, not Guantanamo Bay."

She snorts. "So that power pose is completely natural?"

I uncross my arms, annoyed, and try to look relaxed. She's been in here for less than a minute, and I'm already knocked off kilter. I'm supposed to be in control in this room.

"What can I do for you, Raine?"

She presses her lips together and rolls them, glancing around the room. I follow the trail of her gaze, taking in the sparse bookshelves, the box of tissues, and the stand of mental health leaflets with fresh eyes. Damn it. I need to water my plant. The leaves are browning, curled tragically over the rim of the pot.

"Raine?"

She looks back at me, unruffled. Her features are calm, and despite my better judgement I find myself eager to hear what she has to say. It's rare to get a student in here who's so difficult to read.

"I have some questions. About attraction."

I shift in my chair. "Alright." It's common for students to come here when they're exploring.

"I don't feel it."

"Never?"

She wets her bottom lip. "Not usually."

"That's perfectly normal." I peer at the stand of leaflets, searching for the one about asexuality. Part of me is relieved that she has such an easy issue, one that I'm confident to handle. But a deeper, selfish part of me is disappointed.

So much for a challenge.

"Have you heard of asexuality?" I scan the leaflets as I talk, only glancing at her to check that she's following. She nods, a small frown creasing her forehead as I explain what her lack of attraction could mean. "It's not a problem," I assure her. "You're not lacking in any way. And you can have a fulfilling life and rewarding relationships—"

"I don't think that's it," she interrupts. "Maybe I would have before, but..." she trails off and watches me closely. Seems to make some kind of decision, then states: "I'm attracted to you."

Ah.

Okay.

This is also not uncommon. When students spend their days feeling unseen, unappreciated or misunderstood, to suddenly have someone's undivided attention, even for a few minutes, can be... intoxicating.

"Attraction to authority figures is extremely common. In time, with an appropriate person, I'm sure you will be able to explore—"

"It's not authority figures. It's you. Only one person, in my whole life so far. What is that called?"

She asks it so matter-of-factly. Like she's genuinely interested in the mechanics of attraction, and not trying for some clumsy seduction. Perhaps that's why I humor her, tipping back in my chair and frowning in thought.

"There is something called demisexuality. Where an emotional bond must be formed before sexual attraction can follow. But—"

"But I don't know you."

I smile. "Quite."

There's a moment of quiet. We watch each other, the silence stretching taut between us, and that earlier restlessness is back, prowling under my skin—

Raine throws up her hands. "So that's it? There's no answer?"

"Attraction is complicated. And sexuality is a spectrum. Does there need to be a textbook answer?"

She rolls her eyes, and I stifle another smile. For someone who came for my opinion, she's very prickly when she gets it.

"Look. Some people feel attraction less often. As long as you're not unhappy, I wouldn't stress—"

"I'm not stressed," she interrupts. "I'm curious. Wouldn't you be?"

Yes. Of course I would be. It's easy for me to sit here and lecture, to give her the usual platitudes, but if the roles were reversed, I'd have a thousand questions.

Unfortunately, I can't answer them for her. As soon as she said she wanted me in particular, we crossed a dozen lines.

"Perhaps you could experiment," I say mildly, even as something pinches in my gut. "With people your own age. Look for patterns in which people pique your interest."

The words taste sour in my mouth, and when she scoffs, I can't help but feel relief.

"Do you know any other men like you? Preferably within a ten block radius."

Fuck. I should not find that request gratifying.

"No," I tell her, and grin as she huffs. This is... inappropriate. Too close to flirting. "The library has some books on human sexuality." I stand and gesture for the door. I don't usually end appointments early, but this girl is dangerous. It's too easy to forget she's a student. "If you'd like to talk more, you can book an appointment at reception. With another counselor, Raine."

"Fine." She pushes to her feet, grumbling under her breath, and as she passes me, I get a waft of her scent. She smells like cinnamon and oranges, and I suck in an eager lungful, smoothing my face carefully blank as she looks up at me. "You should water that plant."

The office feels smaller when the door shuts behind her. Colder and dark. I flick an extra lamp on, annoyed. That buzzing energy from earlier is still here, but subdued somehow. Less manic.

The day rolls out before me, endless and dull, and I get the bizarre urge to chase after her. To hear her irritated huff again.

I scrub a hand over my face, then snatch up my coffee mug and head to the break room instead.

She's nothing. Just a dangerous distraction.

3

Chapter Three

"This is really bothering you, isn't it?"

Four days later, Lucy lowers herself to sit cross-legged on the rug beside me in our living room. I've got a gruesome horror movie playing in glorious high definition, a bowl of spiced cashews on the coffee table, and I'm nearly done with embroidering a skull with a pink wig onto my black jacket.

I'm in my freaking element.

"What makes you say that?" I stab the needle through the fabric, savoring the punch then drag of the thread. Whoever thought that Regency ladies were soft and delicate for doing embroidery was an idiot. I bet they were all picturing stabbing the eyes of their enemies.

"Well, you look psychotic."

I glance over, but Lucy's grinning. She nudges my knee with her own, her over-sized sweater dress pooling on her little thighs. Lucy is perfect, a tiny china doll with glossy dark hair, but she's cool enough that she's impossible to resent.

"In what way?"

"The murderous glint in your eye."

I shrug, turning back to my jacket. "That can't be helped. Our brains don't fully develop until our mid-twenties. We're all a bit unhinged."

A hand creeps into my peripheral vision, stealing into my cashew bowl. Lucy slumps back against the sofa, chewing thoughtfully as she watches a man with a hatchet hack up two parked teenagers.

"Why do you like these movies?"

I snort. "Because they're dumb."

"And that's a good thing?"

"Lucy. It's the best." I peer at her, suspicious. "Why the twenty questions? Is this some weird intervention?" Keeley wanders into the living room as I talk, her purple hair damp from the shower and her cheeks still flushed from her run. She drops down to sit on the rug on my other side, sighing and reaching for my cashews. I hiss and smack her hand.

"This *is* an intervention. What do you bitches want?"

Keeley grins, elbowing me in the ribs. Clearly, she hasn't noticed the sharp needle in my hand, or the apparently mad glint in my eye.

"Just checking in on you." Her smile fades. "You've been off lately. Quieter than usual." I don't think of myself as quiet, even though everyone else does. I prefer *reserved*. "The appointment with the guidance counselor didn't help?"

I scrunch up my nose and think about my short discussion with Fraser Drummond. Was it enlightening? Yes. I learned some things. Did it help?

"Nope."

"I'm sorry, Raine."

"Why?" I ask, just to be belligerent. "Is it your fault?" But

Keeley's too good-natured to fall for my bullshit. She stretches her legs out in front of her, kneading her thigh muscles, and carries on talking like I never spoke.

"I don't mean to be insensitive, but does it... does it matter? As long as you're happy—"

"I want to understand," I interrupt. "That's all. I don't like there being secret parts of me that I don't know. It's like..." I trail off and suck my teeth, trying to find a way to explain it. "It's like I've been living in the same house for twenty one years, going in all the rooms and using all the furniture. Then one day I look over and there's a brand new door. A big cupboard I've never seen before. It's freaky."

"So before..." Lucy prompts.

"I never really felt drawn to anyone. And that was fine. It was less to worry about, honestly. But then I finally feel a pull toward someone, just one person, and I want to understand why. Why him? Why now? Am I just making it up in my head? Or has some part of me finally woken up? Will there be others—"

I cut myself off, pressing my lips together. They're right. This is a silly thing to get so fixated on. If it happens, it happens, and if it doesn't, that's fine too.

But I've never been good at letting things drop. I used to get stuck on riddles and brain teasers, obsessing over them for days until I finally solved them.

This is my new riddle. I just need some answers, then I can move on.

Besides. I want to have a groundbreaking career in psychology research. How can I make that happen when I can't even make sense of my own mind?

"I have an idea." Lucy pushes up onto her knees. "Let's go to a bar. We can call it field work. Raine can see if anyone else

16

interests her, and if not, we'll get tipsy and blow off steam."

"I like that second part," Keeley pipes up. She groans as she clambers to her feet, rubbing at her aching muscles. "As long as we find somewhere to sit."

* * *

"How did you know?" I ask, shouting over the din of the bar. We're leaning against the stained mahogany wood, waiting to catch the bartender's eye. "With Beckett. How did you know you liked him?"

A dreamy look floats over Keeley's face and I wish I never asked.

"Gross. Forget it." I flap a hand and spin to survey the room. It's packed in here—it's Friday night in the spring semester, when everyone wakes up from their winter hibernation. It's after 8pm and still light outside, and we're all shuffling bleary-eyed out of our metaphorical caves.

I tug on my black jacket, the embroidered skull leering out from the lapel.

It's show time.

The problem with guys our age is that they're works in progress. Half-made humans. I get it—we're all in the same boat—but it's still really hard to find guys who haven't figured out the importance of bed sheets attractive. The few times I hooked up with someone over the last few years, driven more by curiosity than anything else, exactly one out of three candidates came with fresh bedsheets. The other times, I made them put down a clean towel over their bare mattress and tried not to think too hard about it.

It's a mood killer, that's all I'm saying. Especially if you have barely any mood to begin with.

"Anyone?" Lucy calls from my other side. I sigh and shake my head.

There are the frat boys traveling in noisy packs. The shinier, wealthier guys who study Economics and don't own t-shirts, only button-downs. The scruffy musicians, the troubled poets, the quiet nerds. All of them probably perfectly nice, but I'm unmoved. Cold inside, like the lights are off.

I peer at a few of the women instead, but it's a lost cause. They do even less for me. Which is a pity, because I would bet good money that most of the women know about fresh bed sheets.

"Whatever." I wave a hand, and a cold beer bottle is pushed into my grip. "It's stupid anyway. Let's just hang out."

Keeley and Lucy both smile, relieved, and I herd them to a booth with a sinking feeling in my gut. I tip my beer back, swigging from the cold glass bottle, and slam it on the table with a thud.

It doesn't matter. It doesn't matter.

God, I wish I could switch my brain off.

The bar is so loud I barely hear the chirp of my phone in my pocket. I slide it out, clicking the screen on with a frown. All the people who text me are right here.

It's a college email. I roll my eyes, going to shut the screen off, but a name catches my eye.

Professor F. Drummond.

"Holy shit."

My heart thumps faster in my chest as I open the email, and I note that fact with interest. So he doesn't even have to be here to have an impact? Huh.

It's a forwarded email. There's not a single word from Fraser—only his email signature. And below that, an invitation

18

to an event on Monday in the Psychology Department—one of the professors is giving a talk on sexuality. I scan the details, so eager my breaths are misting up the screen, but my stomach sinks when I reach the bottom.

Staff and graduate students only.

Shit.

I tap back a reply before I can over-think it.

I'm an undergrad. Can you sneak me in?

I hold my breath and wait, but there's no reply. After five full minutes, I slump back against the booth, shoving the phone back in my pocket.

Fine. So he didn't read the fine print. Fraser Drummond doesn't owe me anything. I snatch up my beer and take a long gulp. Lucy and Keeley are chatting about something, laughing easily, and I force myself to tune in. I ask questions, make comments, laugh along, and generally try to masquerade as a human.

When we leave the bar hours later, shivering in the cold breeze, I pull out my phone to order us a ride home.

The little envelope icon makes my heart slam into my rib cage. I click it open with shaking fingers.

His answer is short. To the point. But I whoop and punch the air.

Yes. Meet me in the quad ten minutes before.

Don't be late.

4

Chapter Four

This is a bad idea.

I deliberated for an embarrassingly long amount of time as to whether I should forward the email to Raine at all. I'd thought of her the moment I read the subject line, but my hand had hovered over the mouse, my mind whirring. The water cooler gurgled in the hall outside my office, and still I sat there, carved of stone.

Was this an educational courtesy? The sort of gesture I'd make for any of the students in the Psychology department?

Or was this because of her dry humor? The way her dark, soulful eyes made me feel like I was waking up after a long sleep?

I sent the email to her with one eye screwed shut. My own inappropriate feelings aside, I couldn't deny Raine the chance to learn more about the questions troubling her.

Still. This will be professional. Distant. We're not going to chat.

But when she rounds the corner of the library, waving at me from across the quad, dread slides through my stomach. I stuff my hands deeper in my jacket pockets, nodding at her and watching as she strolls across the paving stones.

She's... eclectic. Her outfit is as jarring as her manner, with a bright yellow scarf looped around her neck and earrings shaped like cacti dangling above the wool. Her black jacket seems normal at first glance, but when she stops in front of me, I notice the embroidered skull wearing a candy pink wig.

Jesus.

What have I gotten myself into?

"Hey, Drummond."

I frown at her. "It's professor."

She cocks her head. "I thought you didn't teach anymore?" There's nothing belligerent about her question, only genuine curiosity, so I find myself grunting and waving toward the Psychology building. The talk is in the largest lecture hall, with rows and rows of cushioned seats rising up like an amphitheater.

The Psychology Department citizens are creatures of comfort. We have padded lecture seats; cozy reading rooms; a secret espresso machine in the staff break room. Whenever I visit Beckett in the Sports Science department, it's like crossing over the Iron Curtain.

At least the shabby Wellness Center keeps me humble.

"Thanks for thinking of me."

I shoot Raine a look, trying to judge what she means by that. Does she mean the professional courtesy I'm insisting this is? Or does she know that I've thought of her more than that? Can she scent it on me like a cat?

It doesn't matter. It changes nothing.

"It's no problem," I mutter. "I was coming either way."

She nods, unoffended, and skips over a glassy puddle at

the edge of the quad. It's early evening, with most of the students long gone and only the pigeons cooing as they roost in the crags of the brick buildings. The Psychology building is drawing a crowd—a steady stream of postgraduate students and department staff, shuffling inside in groups with coffee cups clutched in their hands.

I usher Raine through the entrance, wishing uselessly that she'd tried harder to blend in. That she'd left the skull-in-a-wig jacket at home.

"This way."

She starts to follow the crowd, but I tug on her elbow. She whirls around and blinks up at me, surprised.

"I thought we were going to the talk?"

"We are. But there are no undergrads allowed."

"So how—"

"*This way*, Raine."

She blows out a breath and follows me through the halls, against the flowing current of people. The talk is busy—the speaker is one of the big names in the department, and a topic like sexuality always piques everyone's interest.

There's no way I could smuggle Raine in unnoticed. I tell myself that's why I came up with this scheme—purely to follow through on my offer.

Not so I could watch her closely. See her reactions first hand and answer her questions without my colleagues thinking the worst.

I have no business tutoring this student one-on-one. After tonight, that will be it. We'll draw a line under it.

"I always thought this building was kind of freaky." Raine strolls by my side, hands in her pockets, completely at ease.

"How so?"

She gives me a look. A look that says, *get it together, professor. See what's in front of your face.*

"We have all this funding, right? And everyone always says that the Psychology Department is the nicest one on campus. But all the nice bits are right by the entrance. On the first floor, where visitors see. When you go up a few floors, when you walk through the corridors, it all fades back to normal. Like any other building on campus."

"So?"

Raine snorts. "So, you'd think the Psychology Department would be more self aware. It's all appearances. Putting on a show. Projecting power or prestige or whatever. It's literally a physical manifestation of all these complexes we study in the lectures."

Huh. I peer around the corridors with fresh eyes. Out here, further away from the glossy lobby, the gray carpet is balding and ancient blinds hang on the windows. Raine is right—there's nothing special about this part of the building, and yet somehow, the Psychology department is known for luxury.

"Damn," I mutter, flicking the peeling corner of a poster as we walk past. "The illusion is shattered."

"Sorry," Raine says cheerfully. She doesn't sound sorry at all.

I lead her through the corridors and up two flights of stairs. She follows me gamely, not questioning now that we're walking, and that's a relief too. It's a show of trust, one that I surely haven't earned, and it eases the tight knot in my stomach.

"Here." I come to a stop outside a dark wooden door. It looks exactly the same as every other door in this hallway, except there is no plaque to name the room inside. But Raine nods, eyes bright, and I can't help the smile that tugs my mouth as I push the door open.

There's a pause. A slow breath.

Then: "Holy shit."

Raine laughs quietly, wandering into the projection booth, trailing her fingertips over the shelves of equipment. This is another luxury of the department—a cinema-style projection screen in the biggest lecture theater. It's unmanned—some long-suffering grad student comes up to switch the projector on in advance, but other than that it all runs automatically.

It's pointless, really. But it offers this: a dark room above the lecture theater, separated by tinted glass, and a scattering of cushioned chairs to watch the talk. The sound is muffled, but speakers nestle in the corner of the ceiling, and I wander over and coax them to life. They crackle at first, nothing but static, but with some fiddling we can hear the din in the bigger room.

The talk hasn't started. The crowd are finding their seats, dozens of conversations filling the room with a dull roar. Raine drags two seats right up to the glass, and a shameful part of me is pleased when she puts them close together.

I still drag mine a foot away when I sit down. Raine rolls her eyes but says nothing.

"How did you find this place?" she asks after a minute, playing with a loose thread on her sleeve.

"I used to watch a lot of the talks up here."

She snorts. "Loner much?"

I shrug. She's not wrong.

"I wanted to hear what the speakers had to say. But I didn't want to deal with all..." I wave at the crowds below. "All that."

"You know what I think, Professor Drummond?" She turns, eyebrow quirked. "I think you're kind of a grump."

"A grump?"

"Yeah. I do."

"A grumpy bastard?"

"That's the one."

"I'm wounded."

The din in the room quiets and we both face forward. I catch a glimpse of my own reflection in the glass, the grin stretching my cheeks, and I hurriedly smooth my features blank again.

This is educational. A simple favor. I'd do it for any of the students.

But I can't help but think, as the speaker walks onto the stage, that being alone with the other students doesn't feel dangerous. Being this close to Raine, alone in the dark—that feels like the worst idea I've had in months. Every time I breathe, I catch the faint scent of cinnamon and oranges, and I can hear every rustle as she shifts in her chair. Every soft draw of her breath.

I clear my throat and inch my chair further away.

It's going to be a long evening.

* * *

A hand on my shoulder jerks me awake. Raine leans over me, mouth quirked in a smile as she shakes me gently.

"Hey. The talk's over. Thanks for bringing me." She grins wider. "Hope you liked it."

I sit up straight, rolling my head on my stiff neck. God, what time is it? The crowds are streaming out of the lecture hall below, their conversation buzzing through the tinted glass. I can feel Raine's eyes on me, can practically hear the teasing comments on the tip of her tongue.

I don't want to hear them. Any chance I had of propriety went out the window when I fell asleep in front of her. God, how did that happen? It's dark in here, sure, and the warmth from the projector makes it kind of stuffy. But I've sat up here dozens of times and listened to lectures. I've never fallen asleep before.

How humiliating.

I push to my feet, ignoring Raine altogether. If word got out that I slept in front of her... If someone had come in and found us like that, seemingly close and intimate...

This was such a mistake.

"Let's go." Raine reels back at my tone, but she doesn't argue. She scoops up her jacket and pushes her arms through the sleeves, mouth pursed and her gaze fixed on the floor. Somehow, the sight of that embroidered skull only makes me more irritable, and I sigh as she takes her time, putting the chairs back where she found them.

"If you're in a rush, you could help," she snaps, thudding the chair down on the scratchy carpet. I stride past her and push the door open, checking the corridor before I step out.

This is what I've come to. Sneaking around with a student who has already declared me attractive. Falling asleep next to her in dimly-lit booths; checking the coast is clear before we slip out of the department. According to the Doctorate hanging on my office wall, I'm a man of reasonable intelligence, so how did I get here?

Fuck. Beckett would never let me forget this.

Raine squeezes past me in the doorway and I lurch out of the way, but she just rolls her eyes. To her, I suppose, I fell asleep as one man and woke up as another. A grumpier, jumpier version of myself, who has suddenly remembered the consequences of his actions.

I hope it was worth it, at least.

"Did you enjoy the talk?" Raine glances at me as we stride down the corridor, our footsteps quick. She raises an eyebrow, apparently surprised that I'm even talking to her.

"Yes. It's a shame you slept through it, professor."

So we're back to 'professor'? Suddenly I wish she'd call me Drummond again. But no—that's the problem, the whole reason I should never have sent her that email, and why have I woken up so muddled and furious? I've never been a morning person, but the sun is setting as we push through one of the building's rear exits. There's no good reason for this.

I'm exhausted. That's all it is. I haven't been sleeping well for weeks—months, even. Why else would I fall asleep like that?

"Well." Raine shoves her hands in her pockets and peers up at me. "Thanks again. It was… useful information."

I nod, distracted. Two lecturers from the department walk past on the stone path, waving at me, and I raise a hand awkwardly. They stare at Raine, openly intrigued.

Of course they are. I'm alone with a female student in the evening. We're clearly sneaking out the back of the building. And Raine is undeniably beautiful. Fuck. *Fuck.*

"Don't expect this again," I clip out, putting space between us. "I won't give special treatment." Raine scoffs, shaking her head as she hops down the stone steps to the path.

"Sure. See you around."

She walks off just like that, like we're done, her dark hair swinging in its ponytail, and even though I've been desperate to get this over with since I woke up, I'm suddenly more pissed off than ever. I want to yell after her; I want to jog to catch up and take her elbow. I want to slam my head in the fire door frame.

"Perfect," I mutter, walking slowly down the steps and turning in the opposite direction. I'm going the same way as Raine, actually, but there's no way I'm going to trail after her like some unhinged stalker. I'll do a lap of campus, burn off some of this nervous energy, then head back that way when the coast is clear.

* * *

My apartment is dark when I get home. Silent and cold. Nothing like the stuffy heat of the projection room. I flick a lamp on with a sigh, rolling my head on my stiff neck. I must have slept with it at a weird angle.

God. It's so unlike me. I *never* sleep in public. Hell—I barely sleep in my own bed. I toss and turn for hours, with every snatched moment of sleep a hard won battle.

Something about the warmth of that room, or the dim lighting, or even worse, about *Raine*, must have soothed me for once.

Shit. What a disaster.

The worst part is, I'm still wound tight. Still on edge from her presence, from sitting a few feet from her all alone. My mind knows that I can't go there, but my body clearly didn't get the memo. Just thinking of her now...

My cock hardens painfully.

Well, this is humiliating. Apparently I'm sixteen again, not well into my thirties, and the mere thought of a woman is enough to make a fool of out me. For a moment, I imagine what my brothers would say back in Scotland. How badly they'd take the piss. They'd find this whole situation absolutely hilarious, just like they find *me* little more than a punch line.

I blow out a hard breath, scrubbing both hands down my face.

Alright. Enough self pity.

There are tomorrow's appointments to prepare for; notes to

read over; my abandoned academic work to stare at dolefully. I'm a busy man. People rely on me, rather unfortunately, and even though I often feel utterly unequipped for the experience—distant somehow; cold and wrong—I won't let them down. Without my research, this is all I have to offer.

Raine's face drifts across my mind as I hang up my coat on its peg. She leans forward in my office, calm and unembarrassed, as her glossy dark hair slides over one shoulder. *"I'm attracted to you."*

Ah, shit.

I gave Gideon and Beckett so much crap for this.

I march through my apartment, trying not to think about what I'm about to do. As though if I keep my mind off it, letting my body do its thing, I'm not really there. It's not really happening. I focus on the flashes of rooms through the open doorways instead—my stern-looking office, modeled after my father's; my pristine kitchen with a half-drunk mug of tea on the counter; my living room coffee table strewn with unopened mail. And when I shut myself in the bathroom and switch the shower on, cranking the dial until it runs icy cold, I don't let myself think about *why* I'm taking this plunge.

I'm not attracted to a student. I won't cross any lines.

Liar, says the bulge in my pants.

I unbutton my shirt, glaring at my reflection in the mirror above the sink.

Hypocrite.

5

Chapter Five

Out of the three of us, Lucy has by far the best part time job. Keeley works as a lifeguard in the campus pool, and sometimes covers receptionist shifts at the gym. I reshelve books in the library, dragging squeaky carts of books up and down the stacks. But Lucy works in this cave of wonders—the art supply store. I wander between the tables piled high with sketchpads and pastels; oil paint pots and watercolor sets.

I look, but don't touch. This stuff is Lucy's deal. I'm here for one shelf and one shelf only, tucked away in the textiles badlands in the corner of the store.

"More thread?" Lucy pops up by my shoulder as I browse the jewel-toned little knots. "You've been really getting through them."

It's not a criticism. Lucy blows through art supplies from here like a dealer dipping into her own supply. And her eyes are warm with approval as she elbows me for an answer.

"New design," I murmur, rolling the loose end of an emerald thread between my thumb and forefinger. "For Keeley's sports bag."

My friends are used to finding their clothes and belongings suddenly embroidered overnight. At first, when we'd only just moved in together, I asked permission every time. But they were so freaking excited about it, that we relaxed into this instead—surprise embellishments to make them smile in the mornings.

"You should open a shop," Lucy blurts. "Something online. To sell your designs and custom orders."

I hum and run my fingertips over the bundles of thread, noncommittal, but inside I'm a firework display. Does she really think I'm that good? Surely she wouldn't suggest it to be polite—it's too much work to set something like that up. A *shop*. A way to sell my designs, to make money that doesn't involve haunting the library like some malevolent shadow.

"I'll think about it," I whisper. Lucy whoops and shakes my sleeve. A few tables away, her coworker Dan glances over, tossing an eraser that bounces of Lucy's head.

"Hey! Short stuff. Want to help with this display?"

Lucy wanders off, bickering cheerfully with her coworker. She makes it look so easy—chatting. Getting along with everyone. I'm no outcast, but sometimes I wish I had her *ease*. If I hadn't found Keeley and Lucy early on in our first year...

College could have been much harder.

That's what makes it feel like a cruel joke when she pulls me aside after I pay. She drags me out of earshot, chewing on her bottom lip like she does when she's nervous.

"Listen. Um, before you go. I don't want to make a big deal out of this—"

"Spit it out, Luce." I keep my face carefully blank, casual and unbothered, and that seems to buoy her. Give her some confidence. That makes one of us.

"Sure. Okay. Well you know we had plans for after graduation—staying in the apartment together and looking for jobs in the city?"

"Uh-huh." I don't like where this is going. As far as I know, we *have* those plans. Present tense.

"Well, it's, um." Lucy blows out a harsh breath, then rattles through the rest of it double-time. "Gideon asked me to move in with him. And I want to say yes."

I blink. Lucy stares up at me, eyes wide and worried, and god. What am I supposed to say? *No, you have to put your life on hold for me.* As if.

That doesn't make this suck any less.

"I'll stay for the summer," she says quickly. "So you have time to find a new roommate. Or a new place with Keeley. You know, whatever you like. I won't leave you hanging, Raine. I just wanted to give you a heads up."

She looks so miserable. Stressed and sad, and though I'm no expert, I'm pretty sure big life events are supposed to be happy things. Which means this is about me, about how I'll react.

I thump Lucy gently on the shoulder, and a smile breaks over her face.

"Hey. Congratulations."

"Thank you. Wow! Thanks. I was so worried."

"I'm not that fragile," I say, and it's meant to be teasing, but it comes out kind of harsh. Lucy winces, plucking at her sweater dress, so I wave my paper bag of embroidery supplies. I'm not faking this conversation very well. Time to cut and run, and do better later. "I have to go. Thanks for the shop idea. I'll see you later, okay?"

Lucy nods, her forehead still creased with concern. Shit. I

wheel around and barge out of the art store.

It's fine. This was always going to happen at some time. Who lives with their friends for their whole lives? It was always a temporary plan. Until bigger things happened for us—fancy jobs, relationships, travel.

Maybe I'll pack all my shit and travel the world, funded by an online embroidery store.

Anything to not feel so left behind.

* * *

"What did that backpack ever do to you?"

I squint up from my stone bench, blinking in the dazzling spring sunshine. A man stands a few feet in front of me, hands in his pockets and backlit by the sun, but I don't need to see his face to know who it is. I'd recognize his low, precise voice anywhere. And unlucky for him, he's the last man I want to see.

"It asked me stupid questions," I clip out, stabbing my needle through the thick canvas. Keeley's sports bag will have to wait—I had way too many thoughts racing through my mind when I stepped out of the art store, and a spot on my backpack that I've been saving for emergencies just like this. There's so much embroidery on this old backpack that you can barely see the original gray fabric.

Professor Drummond whistles softly. "Bad day, Raine?"

"No." I yank hard on the thread. *Too* hard. It nearly snaps and ruins all my work. "Great day, actually. The sun is shining. I bought brand new thread. And I managed to avoid dumbass conversations right up until you arrived."

The professor checks his watch. "Nearly midday."

"See?" I stab the needle through the canvas again, my tongue prodding my cheek. "Not a bad run."

He lingers for a second, not saying anything. What am I, a zoo animal? I open my mouth to tell him to piss off, but he beats me to it, speaking horrifically gently.

"I could make an appointment for you at the Wellness Center. If you're having a hard time—"

I hold the needle up toward him, the sunshine glinting off the metal.

"Stop. Shut up. Don't even say it. Don't think I won't stab you just because you're a professor."

He laughs. He actually tilts his head back and laughs, and *why* does that make my stomach swoop? I scowl down at my design, at the ginger tabby cat sharpening its claws on the zipper line.

It's pretty good.

By the time I finally look up, Professor Drummond is gone. I peer around the quad, stomach sinking, but there's no flash of copper hair. Guess I scared him off, too. And when I turn back to the half-stitched design in my lap, my face is rigid from trying not to crumple.

"Here." Five minutes later, a take-out coffee cup is thrust in my face. Fraser watches me from the other end of it, mouth twitching in amusement. And I'm still pissed off at him, damn it, still annoyed he was so rude, but the scent of freshly roasted coffee makes my mouth water.

"This means nothing." I pluck the cup from his hand, our fingers brushing. He nods and sits down beside me, a safe distance between us on the bench.

"Noted."

He cradles his own coffee cup against his chest, like some injured baby bird. It's kind of funny, and I can't help the quirk to my mouth when he looks over.

"So what's really going on?"

Jeez. Can't catch a break. I shake my head, ready to tell him to go, coffee or no, but he holds up a palm in surrender.

"Alright, alright. We don't have to discuss it." But apparently he didn't get his own memo, because he immediately asks: "Is it the attraction thing?"

Is it me, or does he sound kind of hopeful? I shake my head.

"No. Honestly, that's kind of the last thing on my mind." And it's true. It's still a maddening puzzle, something I want to figure out, but there are more important things going on. More immediate concerns.

Like where I'm going to live after the summer. And who with. Will Keeley move in with Beckett? As soon as I consider it, I know the answer. *Yes.*

My closest friends are moving on with their lives, with relationships and big plans for their careers, and I don't even really know what I want to do next. I'm getting left behind.

"If it's to do with your classes, maybe I could help."

I glance over. "Are you always such a fixer?"

His eyebrows shoot up, but he tilts his head, actually considering the question. And after a long pause, he says quietly, "Yes."

"Maybe you should deal with your own crap first. You know, eyes on your own page."

I'm being belligerent, but he simply says, "Maybe." And he's not angry—if anything, he's faintly amused. Like I've got him nailed, and he appreciates the irony. I lean over, fixing a sympathetic look on my face.

"If it's to do with your personality, maybe I could help."

He laughs again, the sound sudden and loud—shocked out of him by my rudeness. And his pale blue eyes twinkle as he swigs from his coffee cup, the column of his throat working as he swallows.

Damn. My mouth runs dry, and I look back at my lap, suddenly flustered. No matter how many times this man pisses me off, he still has this effect on me. Still makes my skin flush hot and my blood pump faster.

"You know where to find me, Raine. Let me know if I can help." He stands and strides off without another word. I watch him walk away, sadly enraptured by the curve of his ass in his dress slacks.

Such a cliche. I hoped for more from myself. But I guess there are worse vices than thirsting after a professor.

Even one who blows hot and cold like he does, lashing out at one moment and bringing me coffee the next. He didn't even call me out for not thanking him like I should, content to sit by me and be insulted instead.

I wonder what that intensity would be like in other scenarios. All that pent up passion and frustration, let loose. I snatch up my coffee and take a long swig, watching a puff of cloud drift overhead.

Doesn't matter. I'll never find out.

6

Chapter Six

Something is bothering Raine.

I shouldn't know that so instinctively. And it definitely shouldn't prey on my mind. But here I am, prowling through the Sports Science department, desperate to avoid my cold, silent office with its leaflets and dying plant. The longer I stay in there, the more my mind spins in circles—worrying about Raine, worrying about the *fact* that I'm worrying about Raine, wondering if I'll ever publish another research paper again.

You know. Fun thoughts. So I took off, striding out through the Wellness Center lobby the second I finished with the day's appointments, throwing a rushed goodbye at the receptionist Maggie over my shoulder. It's only 4pm. I still have shit to do, but if I sit in that room any longer, I'll lose my damn mind.

So I'm here. In the Sports Science wasteland; the building where ninety per cent of the funding goes towards shiny machines specifically designed to torture the human body. Beckett lives for this stuff—brand new ways to hone muscles that no ordinary person is even aware of. Ways to break down lactic acid, or simulate running on top of a mountain, as though that is a good thing somehow.

The downside to the department spending all their funding on equipment is that the building itself is two steps from a slum. The carpet is balding; the windows are smudgy; the walls are marked, their paint chipped.

There's something honest about it though, I suppose. Unpretentious. Since Raine pointed out the way the Psychology department postures for visitors, then becomes shabbier behind the scenes...

Well. The Sports Science building isn't so bad.

Since it is still the afternoon, with practical sessions and lectures happening all around, students mill through the hallways. I push through with ease, relying on the naturally pissed off expression on my face. *Resting bitch face*, Gideon calls it. And a knot tightens in my chest when I find Beckett's office door propped open, his desk suspiciously clean. Because the man behind the desk isn't Beckett, and I remember with dismay that he *left*, weeks ago, and holy shit, I'm going insane. I actually forgot that my friend left his job. That he works on the coast now, hours away.

I'm the one who told him to resign, for god's sake. I stare at the much cleaner office, jerking slightly when the occupant calls out.

"Are you looking for someone?"

I shake my head mutely. It's rude, but I stride away, in no mood to explain to a stranger that the man I'm looking for is several hours' drive away, and that I'm going senile in my thirties.

Gideon is gone too. They both left this year, packing in their careers to be with their forbidden girlfriends. I judged them both fairly harshly at the time—it takes years of work to become a professor, years of blood, sweat and tears—but now that I can't even sit in my office for five minutes without obsessing about Raine... I understand them both a little better.

What would they say, if they saw me like this? If they knew I was just as bad as them both—worse really, in my hypocrisy?

No. That's not right. I'm not as bad as them, because I haven't touched her. Even when she came to me and declared her attraction, even when we sat side by side in that projection room—I kept things professional.

As professional as they can be when you fall asleep in front of a near stranger.

With Beckett gone, there's no one left for me on campus to go and rant at. To prod at for my own selfish amusement. For years, now, it's been the three of us—Gideon, Beckett, and I.

They've moved on. Left me behind.

God, I'm morbid today. Enough of this crap. I burst out of the Sports Science building doors and march across the quad. Coffee is the answer. Coffee is what I need. And if I glance around as I walk, hoping for a glimpse of some furious embroidery as I go, well, that's between the devil and me.

She's not here anyway.

So. That's good.

* * *

No, it's *not* good. The coffee I gulp down greedily from the coffee shop—I barely taste it as it burns my tongue. I'm as restless as ever, and now urged on by caffeine as I stride around campus like a tiger prowling its cage in a zoo.

If I were studying myself, I'd think myself the perfect subject.

A clearly unhinged individual, with a no doubt fascinating psychological makeup.

It's cold comfort. I push through the library doors, determined to find a better distraction.

I find one, but it's not exactly what I had in mind. When I lunge up the stairs to the third floor, taking the steps two at a time, *she's* here, dragging a metal cart piled high with books through the stacks. Headphones are lodged in her ears. She nods gently in time with whatever music she's listening to, wrapped up in her own little world.

I walk over to her without thinking, cutting a shameless beeline through the stacks. Desks line the walls on either side of the floor, but their occupants are bent over their books or tapping away at laptops. Those who aren't studying are flirting shamelessly, whispering in each other's ears and moving to sit in laps.

Good. Hopefully no one will notice my little display.

"Raine?" I murmur her name, reluctant to draw attention, but she doesn't hear me through her music. She hums under her breath, delightfully out of tune, and I can't help my grin as I tap her shoulder. "Raine."

She turns to me with a look of sheer disdain—the look she must save for students who bother her at work—but I'm relieved to see it melt into a surprised smile. I can see the exact moment she remembers she's annoyed at me, smoothing that smile away with effort.

Too late, Raine. I saw it. Can't take it back.

"What's up?" She tugs one earphone out by the cable, leaving one in as a clear *fuck you*. My grin widens and I look down at the cart.

"I have a library-related query."

"Oh?"

Is that disappointment in her eyes? This is too much fun. When I came here for a distraction, this is not what I had planned. I'm supposed to be staying far away from her, pushing her out of my mind, not hounding her at her job to tease her into smiling.

"Yes." She's wearing a forest green sweater today, one that hugs her curves and shows the swell of her hips. It's surprisingly demure for the girl who embroiders pink-wigged skulls onto her jackets. Does she have a dress code at work? Seems kind of intense for reshelving library loans. "I need help finding a book."

She blows out a hard breath, fluttering the strands of hair hanging in her face. Most of her thick, black hair is teased back into some kind of braid, but a few escapees hang around her eyes and tickle her cheeks.

"There are desks for that. With librarians."

"I'm familiar with the concept."

Raine rolls her eyes. "Go and find one, then." She moves to grab her cart again, but I step closer.

"I don't want their help. I want yours."

This is dangerous territory. So risky, so reckless, but I can't regret those words when interest flares in her eyes. She glances around the large room too, scanning the students at the desks, like it's just occurred to her too that we have an audience.

"What's the book?" she murmurs.

"Blackwell's Principles of Psychology," I invent immediately. It's a fairly unconvincing title, and she eyes me shrewdly, but says nothing as she drops the book in her hand back onto the pile. I expect her to take her cart somewhere, to insist on finishing her task, but Raine shoves her hands in her jeans pockets and strides away, abandoning it in the aisle.

"This won't cause you trouble, will it?" I catch up with her easily.

"Of course not. I'm helping a professor, remember?"

Right. A professor. Not an unhinged madman, chasing after his ill-advised crush. I should undo this all now, fake a phone call and run for the quad, but god help me, I fall into step beside her. The psychology section is on this floor, further back and tucked in a corner.

I let her lead me there.

"Blackwell's Principles of Psychology," Raine repeats flatly as we step between the stacks.

"Yep."

"Sounds kind of broad."

I shrug. "It's good to cover the basics."

The look she gives me is a mix of amusement and withering condescension, and the two together is oddly thrilling. I lean back against the shelves, watching her hungrily when her back is turned and no one can see my sins. Raine crouches to read titles; straightens up and tips back her head to read the highest shelves. This near, with no one watching me, I can fully appreciate the curve of her waist. The way her dark braid dangles between her shoulder blades.

Is her hair heavy? Does it ever bother her? I firmly push the image of tugging her by the braid out of my mind before it can take root.

Raine inches along slowly, her breaths soft in the small space between the stacks. It's strangely quiet, tucked away here. Like we're in another world.

Across the room, someone coughs.

"You're sure it's Blackwell?"

I hum. "Maybe Blackstone."

She sighs and trudges back along the shelves.

"Or Brentworth," I put in. "Definitely something with a 'B'."

Raine scoffs and wheels around to face me, her mouth tugging up at the corner. "You're messing with me, professor."

"It's Drummond, actually." Her eyes flash, and for a split second I think I've done it. Crossed an invisible line and dragged her with me; shattered the uncomfortable stalemate between us. But then Raine looks down, shaking her head with a smile, and even if she's not annoyed anymore, she's not looking at me like I'm edible either.

When she first looked at me with outright hunger, I was annoyed. It made me nervous, and more than that, it felt lowering somehow. Crude.

Now I think I'd do several terrible things if it coaxed her to look at me like that again. With bold, unabashed lust.

"I should get back to work," Raine says quietly. She goes to squeeze past me but I place my hands on her shoulders, pinning her in place.

"Wait a moment." I tug the headphone out of her ear. "Tell me what's wrong."

"You're not in the Wellness Center now, Drummond."

Drummond. Finally. I knead her shoulders without thinking, massaging the knots in her muscles.

"In the quad. When you were murdering that backpack. You seemed upset."

"Well spotted. Did they teach you that in postgrad?"

"Raine."

She gusts out a sigh. When she speaks, her words are mumbled. Barely allowed to squeeze past her lips.

"Lucy's moving in with Gideon."

43

I frown. "So?"

"So we'll need a roommate. If Keeley doesn't move straight in with Beckett—which, come on. Is clearly going to happen. So *I* need to figure out a new plan. Somewhere to live; some career ideas. And it just makes me wonder why I'm staying in this city at all, what's even left here for me, and—"

She cuts herself off, scowling at the floor. I don't think I've ever heard her say so much in one go. It's all stuff that I hear every day as a guidance counselor, though I have enough self-preservation instinct not to say it.

"You'll figure it out," I murmur instead. "Everyone's a mess after college. You'll blunder around a bit and make some mistakes, but you'll get there eventually."

Raine scoffs, shrugging my hands off her shoulders. "Like you did? How's your research going, *professor?*"

We stand there for a breathless moment, the silent stretching taut between us. Raine opens her mouth to speak again, but I back towards the end of the aisle.

"Good point. Excellent counter argument, Raine."

"Fraser—"

I stroll back across the library floor with my hands in my pockets and my face relaxed. If any of these industrious students looked over, they'd see a calm professor. Cool and collected.

Only Raine sees the truth. It's not much consolation.

7

Chapter Seven

I scroll through the apartment listings, trying not to lose the will to live. Every one bed or studio in my budget looks like something in Chernobyl. I swear there's an actual rat in one of the photos. A live rat, practically waving its diseased paw at the camera.

I slam the laptop shut and toss it on the sofa cushion beside me. There must be other decent roommates in this city. Sure, they won't be my best friends, but there must be people who aren't criminally insane and who won't steal my yogurt.

"Any luck?" Keeley gasps from the floor, mid-way through some horrendous plank exercise. Her cheeks are flushed bright red, and her jaw is gritted, but she won't give in. Keeley is a fighter.

Me, I'd flop on that rug in two seconds flat. A plank? Please. When am I ever going to need that?

"A few good ones," I lie, picking at my chipped nail polish. Lucy and Keeley already feel so guilty for bailing on me. As soon as I brought it up with Keeley, she got all fidgety and I *knew.*

It's as I feared. They're both moving on. We have the rest of this semester, a month of summer, then they're gone. *Poof.* Leaving me with the mutant rat.

Whatever. I'll find something good. Somewhere that is more distressed-chic than just plain distressed. Fraser's comforting words float across my mind, the way he kneaded my aching shoulders as he told me it would all be okay.

Then I had to be a dick. It's pathological at this point. I could sense an incoming feeling, and my defenses snapped up. Still, he probably didn't deserve that—and I don't buy his unaffected act for a second.

I hurt his feelings. Or pissed him off. Probably both. I dig out my phone and scroll through my emails.

If he was a normal man and not a professor, I'd have his number by now. A way of calling him. But I don't—all I have is his email signature. With the phone number for his office, and his work email.

Does the college read through staff emails? I chew on the inside of my cheek as I type, playing it safe just in case.

To: Professor F. Drummond
From: Raine Laghari
Subject: Blackwell's Principles of Psychology
Hi Professor,
I found the book you wanted from the library. You were right about Blackwell's ideas on optimism.
Shall I drop it by your office tomorrow?
Raine

I drum on the arm of the sofa as I wait. He might not even see it tonight—it's the evening, damn it. He probably has cool plans or a hot date with a non-petulant woman.

The grin spreads over my face when my phone pings. His reply is short, but I still hiss and punch the air.

"What is it?" Keeley wheezes from her plank. "Have you found a place?"

"Nope." I tune her out, reading his email again.

To: Raine Laghari
  From: Professor F. Drummond
  Subject: Blackstone's Philosophies of Psychiatry
  Hi Raine,
  That's excellent news. The book is extremely hard to get hold of.
  By all means, bring it by my office. There will be a spare coffee on
my desk at 2pm.
  Yours,
  Prof. Drummond

* * *

I knock on his office door at 1.55pm. It's over-eager, yes—fairly shameless. But then so was emailing him last night. And he sure as hell didn't seem to mind, replying back to me within what felt like seconds.

I rap on the wooden door, peering around the corridor. The Wellness Center is a depressing building. Kind of ironic, really. It's all sickly gray walls and scruffy carpet and water coolers teetering to one side. The sound of my knock echoes around the empty hall, but there's no one nearby to hear it.

Heat creeps into my cheeks.

It's coffee, that's all. A chat. Nothing to blush about; nothing to sneak around over. If anyone were to poke their heads around Fraser's door, they'd find a professor and student talking politely. About classes or something.

Right.

"Come in." Fraser's voice drifts through the door. He sounds faintly amused, like he's gratified that I came early. I suddenly wish I'd done another nervous lap around the campus.

"It's raining outside," I say breezily as I push through the door. "Didn't want to get soaked."

Fraser smirks at me from his desk chair. He nods at his office window.

"Liar."

Okay, so it's sunny. I didn't think that through. But who can blame me when he looks like that? Fraser Drummond is all long limbs and toned muscles; coppery hair and sharp cheekbones. When he leans back in his chair and smolders at me like that, of course I say dumb shit.

"I'm sorry about yesterday." I won't talk in circles about this. I'd rather hash it out now and be up front with each other. My footsteps thump on the horrible carpet as I cross to the desk, flopping into the spare chair and reaching for my coffee. Steam curls from the opening in the lid, snaking toward the ceiling.

"What about it?"

I guess Fraser didn't get the straightforward gene. I roll my eyes and shift in my seat, trying to get comfortable.

"The part where you tried to be nice to me and I insulted you in return."

"Ah. That part."

"Yeah." I peel the lid off the coffee and blow on the foam. Cappuccinos today. "I'm sorry about that."

Fraser shrugs and smiles, and it's like the sunshine beaming through the window.

48

"No problem. You didn't say anything untrue."

"Don't you see how that's worse?"

Fraser snorts. "I suppose." He nods at the drink in my hand. "Is that alright?"

It's hot. It's caffeinated. It's free of charge. *Duh*, it's okay. It's delicious, actually.

It's surprisingly easy, being here with him. I guess I expected the same awkwardness as my first visit: him prickly and standoffish, and me going all cold and stiff in response. But maybe it's the way he leans back and grins, easy and warm, or maybe it's all in my head, but this time feels so much better.

"How's your research going?" Fraser asks suddenly. As though he was thinking of our first meeting here too. "Have you found anyone else who piques your interest?" He asks the question so casually, anyone would think he didn't care. Like he was chatting about the weather. But *I* see the muscle tic in his jaw as he glances down, nudging a stapler so that it's parallel to his keyboard.

"I haven't been looking for the last few days. Kind of busy with the apartment stuff."

Fraser huffs. "That's not a 'no'."

It's my turn to grin. "Are you jealous, professor?"

The look he gives me would wither shrubs on the spot. "That would be inappropriate."

"That's not a 'no' either," I mutter, hiding my smirk in my coffee cup. I take a long swig, savoring the hot spread of coffee over my tongue, but when I place the cup down with a hollow thud, Fraser is staring out of the window. He looks lost again. Sad and unsettled, like he did after the projection booth.

You know, right before he was a complete asshole. I hold up my palms, ready to ward off his bile.

"I know, I know. I was just messing with you. Don't worry, I'm not going to try anything. I won't lunge at you over the desk."

He looks back at me, a slight frown creasing his forehead.

"That's the problem. I don't think I'd stop you if you did."

Heat flushes under my skin. I sit up straighter in my chair. Again, just like in the library, there's the feeling of something stretching taut between us. A tether of some kind. Something about to *snap*.

"Good thing you have more sense," Fraser says, and the moment is over. He drums his fingers on the desk, mouth twisted, and I kick blindly under the table. The *oof* he makes when my sneaker connects with his ankle is perfect.

"Lighten up, Drummond. Don't you listen to your own guidance counselor bullshit?" I stand before he can answer, dancing out of the way of his answering kick. There's a half full bottle of water on his desk, and I snatch it up before crossing to his houseplant. It's slumped over and sallow, wasting away in the shadowy corner, far from the sunshine and clearly not watered enough. I tuck the water bottle under my arm, grab the heavy ceramic pot by the rim, and drag it across the carpet.

"Raine." Fraser appears at my elbow, nudging me out of the way. "For fuck's sake." He lifts it easily. "Where exactly is my plant fleeing to?"

I nod at the window. "To a better life."

"Was there anything else?" Fraser grouses once we've settled the plant in the sunshine and I've tipped the water onto the parched soil. I grab a tissue out of the box on his desk, wiping gently at the dusty leaves. "Do you want to update my computer? Overhaul my schedule? Rearrange the leaflets?"

I throw a doubtful look over my shoulder. "Trust me, no one

cares about the leaflets."

"Well, if you've finished your coffee…"

He's kicking me out. Probably has brooding to do. Well, I'm not ready to go yet. Not with my coffee half drunk, and definitely not with all this nervous energy buzzing through my veins. I stride to the door before he can stop me, pausing before I spin the look.

"Raine." It's a warning. Maybe a plea. I turn and lean back against the door, flattening my palms on the wood. Over here, with several feet between us, I can *feel* the path his eyes take as they roam down my body. Over my baggy Garfield t-shirt that I sleep in sometimes, tucked in to a pair of skinny high-waisted jeans. Over my thick, black hair, left loose for once, tumbling over my shoulders in glossy waves.

"Like what you see?" I whisper.

"*Raine.* You know I can't do this."

"Don't, then." I wet my lip. "Let me."

For all his high-and-mightiness, Fraser Drummond does not put up much of a fight. I'd tease him for it, but this moment already feels fragile. Like a sparkly soap bubble—one rough touch, and it will pop. I back him into his desk chair slowly, carefully, my eyes fixed on his. He watches me back as he goes, hungry and tortured.

The backs of his legs hit the chair.

"Sit," I tell him.

He sits.

I stand for a moment, considering my options. Soaking in the sight of him, so pliable in this moment. I think I could ask anything of him right now and he'd say yes. He'd bend me over the desk and fuck me from behind; he'd let me crawl under the table and take him in my mouth. Both are tempting images, enough to make my core pulse, but I think they might break him. If not during, then after.

So I save that stuff for later. When I'm alone and need something to imagine. Or when he's finally come around to this thing between us. For now, I place a hand on his shoulder, and lower myself into his lap.

Fraser snorts, his arms winding tight around me. The puff of his breath tickles my hairs against my neck.

"You locked the door so we could cuddle?"

"Is that a problem?" I wriggle slightly, grinding down on the hard length beneath my thighs. "I can debauch you more if you like."

"No." There's a pause, then warm lips press against my temple. "No, this is fine."

I've never been much of a cuddler. Whenever Keeley reels me into a hug, or Lucy squeezes me from behind, I go along with it in good humor. But I never initiate.

This is what all the fuss must have been about. Strong sturdy legs beneath me, toned arms caging me against a broad chest. The scrape of his chin on the side of my hair, and the *scent* of him. Soap and old books and fine leather. And when Fraser speaks, the words rumble right through his chest, vibrating into my body in turn. We could have whole conversations like this, with the volume on mute—just rumbling back and forth at each other.

A broad palm rubs circles on my back. I melt against him a little more.

"Your guidance counselor techniques are awesome," I murmur against his throat. It bobs as he swallows, the motion brushing the tip of my nose.

"Thank you. Sometimes I wonder if it's worth it, getting all those football players into my lap."

I snort. He hugs me tighter. "They must flatten you. Poor professor."

I wait for him to say something else. To tease me back, or to draw out this joke, but he's silent. Finally relaxed, for the first time since I've known him. Professor Drummond cradles me against his chest, breathing in the scent of my hair, and just... *is.*

"I feel like a teddy bear," I whisper after a while.

Fraser hums. "You are."

"Should I be offended by that?"

My whole world rocks as he shrugs. "Probably."

I weigh my next question for a long time. Until sounds drift through the door to the corridor—people coming and going from their appointments. Our stolen moment is nearly up.

"Will you do something for me?"

"I'm certain I don't have the will power to tell you no."

"Shut up. Will you kiss me?"

He shifts beneath me, awkward again, and my stomach swoops.

"Raine..."

"You're the only person I'm drawn to." I sit up straight, clutch a handful of his shirt and thump his chest. "The only person I want this way. *Please.* Just show me what it's like. I want to know how it feels when it's with someone you really want. You're the only person who can teach me that." I nip the tip of his nose gently. "Come on, Drummond."

The sigh that gusts out of him must have been dredged up from his shoes. I swear he ages five years before my eyes. But then he nods, the movement jerky, and juggles me in his arms as he teases a hand free and cups my cheek.

Light blue eyes lock onto mine. They're so pale, like the spring skies outside. The pad of his thumb traces my cheekbone, back and forth.

"I can't give you everything you deserve, Raine."

"I'm not asking for all that. Just a kiss."

His eyes close briefly, like he's in pain, but then his mouth comes down on mine. It's gentle, so achingly gentle, and I kiss him back harder, trying to urge him on. I want the savage Fraser, the one with the vicious glint in his eye. And when I tug his bottom lip between my teeth, I finally get him.

"Raine," he growls, grabbing my hips and thrusting up against me. It's dizzying, all the desire thrumming through me. I ought to be making mental notes, cataloguing this experience, but when he slides his tongue into my mouth I barely remember my own name. Professor Drummond kisses me like he's punishing me. Almost cruel in his desire.

It's *delicious.*

"God," I gasp when we break apart for breath. We're still clinging close, fighting to get nearer to each other. "I think I get it now."

"Oh? Let me remind you one more time."

His mouth crashes down on mine and I sway under the force of his kiss. Fraser is not just teaching me something—he's setting out to *ruin* me. Selfish bastard. But you know what? I'm not even mad. This is what I want—that unstoppable hunger. The knowledge that he couldn't let me off his lap right now if he tried.

The knock on his door has us leaping apart.

"Just a moment," Fraser calls, voice rough. I pull my clothes back in order in record time, grabbing my backpack and my coffee cup and smoothing my palms over my hair. Fraser scans me once and nods before spinning the lock and opening the door in one motion, the suspicious noise mostly covered. A guy my age blinks at me through the doorway, glancing between us.

"Oh, sorry. I thought I had a session—"

"You do, Michael." Fraser clear his throat and smiles at me politely. It's jarring after just having his tongue in my mouth. "Raine was just leaving."

Ugh. Fine. I know I need to go, but does he have to say it like that? I fight the urge to roll my eyes as I stomp past him out the door.

"See you, professor," I call over my shoulder, just to get him back. "Thanks for the leaflets."

There's a strangled cough, then his door thuds closed.

8

Chapter Eight

When I was a reckless teenager back in Scotland, I rode a motorbike. It was the source of much mockery from my brothers, but I deemed it worth it for the feel of cold, salty air whipping my cheeks. For the power of the engine roaring beneath me; to feel the lurch of the world left and right as I rounded bends in the road.

A cliche, obviously. But so many of the best things are. And I fucking loved that bike.

When I eventually crashed, as one is almost bound to do in a rain-drenched country like Scotland, it happened—cliche or no—in slow motion. I don't mean that everything slowed to a painful crawl and my whole adolescent life flashed before my eyes and the very sounds around me deepened and morphed. I mean that my brain had time to realize what was happening, to contemplate all the terrible ways this could pan out, to fully anticipate all the *pain* headed my way. And I was helpless to stop it. A horrified observer in one of the worst moments of my life.

Anyway. This feels a bit like that. Minus the squeal of tires and the sickening crack of bone.

Certainly minus the godawful road rash.

But every moment spent with Raine is a slow motion bike crash. I can see the fallout headed my way: disgrace. Scandal. Bottomless shame. But I can't help myself. As weak as that makes me, as weak as I called Gideon and Beckett for the same thing—*I can't stop this.* It's bigger than me somehow. An unstoppable pull.

That will all sound very good, of course, when I'm dragged before the college board. Really romantic. I groan and scrub both hands over my face, pacing up and down my empty apartment.

Why? Why did she have to highlight how cold and hollow my life is? I was comfortable before. Or at least… sleepwalking.

Now I'm itching and aware. My clothes scrape over my skin; my apartment echoes and its appliances rattle until my eyes cross. There's no refuge from this—my office is even more depressing, now that the faint scent of her lingers in the air, and my plants leaves are perking up and craning towards the window. And going to a bar and drinking alone is so… grim.

I refuse to be a national stereotype.

My phone buzzes in my pocket and I snatch it like a lifeline. There's a brief pinch of disappointment when it's not Raine—*she doesn't even have your number, idiot*—but Beckett's name on the screen is a welcome distraction.

"Yes?" I bark, pressing the phone to my cheek. "What's going on? Please, god, tell me something is happening."

Beckett splutters a laugh. "Hey, man. I had no idea you missed me this much."

I grind the heel of my palm into one eye. "Well, I do. I'm pining, asshole."

"Come for a drink, then," he says easily. Beckett is one of those people: friendly. Gregarious. *Fun.* I used to mock him for it, but now I think I need his easy presence more than anything. If I don't find a distraction soon, I'll do something I regret.

Like send Raine filthy nothings from my college email address. Like go through the student record for her phone number.

Very unwise things.

"Where?" I'm too on edge to form sentences. I'm lucky Beckett is used to me, and that he's a better person than I am.

"Donovan's?"

"I'll be there in twenty." I hang up before I can say anything else. Anything pathetic like *can the girls come please?* Jesus Christ, I am supposed to be a grown man. Raine has ruined me. I'll never recover.

*** *** ***

She's here.

She's *fucking here,* and is my own friend conspiring against me? But of course he's not—Beckett grins and claps me on the shoulder when I arrive, calling to the bartender and placing my order from memory. He has no reason to think that I'm spiraling into madness. That I'm drooling over a student.

He couldn't really judge me, but that's not much comfort. It's not like I've confided in him about this. I've just shut myself away in the silent gloom of my apartment, to steep in my own self-loathing.

"The girls have a booth," Beckett tells me, steering me across the bar. It's a Wednesday night, so the crowds are less thick. The energy is less manic, too—less *let's get messy*, and more *let's wind the hell down*. Keeley, Lucy and Raine all sit with Gideon, clustered around a booth tucked away from the bar.

Lucy's pressed against Gideon's side. As we approach, she takes a sip of his drink. And Beckett slides in beside Keeley, pulling her close until they're plastered together.

I stare down at Raine. At the empty seat beside her. She stares back, quirking an eyebrow.

"Problem, professor?"

Gideon bursts out a laugh. "You don't have to call him that here."

I clench my jaw and slide into the booth. Raine shuffles over to make room, giving me a wide berth, and somehow that's worse. I want her squished up against me, damn it. I want to feel the heat of her; to smell the scent of her hair.

Raine clears her throat, stuffing her hands beneath her thighs. She's wearing the same dark skinny jeans as yesterday, but the Garfield t-shirt is gone. Replaced by a baggy old tourist t-shirt for a defunct theme park, tied in a knot at her hip.

Once the others are chatting, distracted, I reach below the table and tug at that knot. She elbows me off, her lips pressed in a line to hide her smile.

Okay. This isn't so bad. It's a slow motion bike crash, yes, but the scenery is incredible. And something tells me Raine is worth that crunching pain of impact. If I'm lucky, maybe she'll stick around to peel me off the road.

"Good day, Drummond?" Her dark eyes sparkle.

"It's Fraser, actually."

Her mouth twitches. "Make up your mind."

It's been just over a day since I saw her last. Since she sat in my lap and asked for a kiss. How did I keep even these last few shreds of my dignity? Seeing her again sends an immediate hit of pleasure and relief through my system. This must be how addicts feel.

Is there a leaflet for this?

"Terrible day." I lean an inch closer, lowering my voice so I'm speaking just to her. "No one gatecrashed my office today. And my plant looks annoyingly healthy."

"How irritating." Raine smirks, and it takes me far too long to realize the others are staring. Silence hangs around the booth, Gideon's mouth parted in a rueful half-smile, and Beckett looks downright scandalized.

Hypocrite, I want to yell. As far as he knows, I'm just flirting a little. He doesn't know about what happened in my office yesterday. Meanwhile, he took Keeley to bed before he ever confessed to anything.

Ugh. I'm a wreck. An asshole catching at straws. And Raine must sense the cloud of self-loathing settling over my shoulders, because she inches away from me and pretends nothing has happened.

"Keeley! Have you and Beckett found a place for after the summer?"

The buzz of conversation fills the booth, and I've escaped this time. Except for the calculating glances that both Beckett and Gideon keep throwing my way. And Keeley's sudden, bubbly excitement, partnered with Lucy's wry amusement.

Fuck. They know. They *know.* Maybe not that something's happened already, but the truth must be etched on my face. I want Raine badly, more than I want to be respectable. More than my career, already half in ruins.

Hell, I don't even *like* being a professor. Isn't that why I'm hiding in the Wellness Center, masquerading as a guidance counselor? Isn't that why I paused all my research, suddenly so sick of it that I couldn't stand another minute?

What exactly am I trying to protect here? I swig from my bottle, scowling down at the scratched wood. And I barely catch what the others are saying, until Lucy's bright suggestion finally registers, setting off sirens.

"Raine, you should see if you like anyone here." She traces her fingertip over the rim of her glass, leaning forward with a delicate flush on her cheeks. Little Lucy can't exactly hold her drink. "There are loads of cute guys here tonight."

"Wait, what?" Gideon raises his eyebrows, feigning insult, and I don't want to watch their flirting right now. Don't want to see their obvious, almost sickening love. I stare at Raine instead, gauging her reaction as my heart thumps faster in my chest.

Raine shrugs one shoulder, her face blank. "I'm not in the mood."

Lucy's eyes flick to mine, then back to Raine. "Are you sure? Just chat to one guy, Raine. If you feel nothing, that's information too."

Raine pauses, and shit. That's how I'd try to persuade her too. Raine is obsessed with gathering data. And though I find that adorable most of the time, right now I wish she'd care less about trying to understand everything.

"You don't have to," I say as casually as I can manage, and they're looking at me again. I push on, voice hoarse. "None of the other students I've spoken to about these types of things find forcing the matter helpful."

Her eyes darken. I've said the wrong thing. What, by comparing her to my other students? She *is* a student. And though she's more to me now, the first time she came to me about this, she did so for advice. From a guidance counselor. Not from *me*.

My thoughts tangle and race, the right thing to say slipping out of reach, and then she's standing and shuffling past me out of the booth.

"Be back in a moment," she murmurs, and I dig my fists into the underside of the table to keep from reaching for her. Reeling her back in. Back to my lap, her face pressed into my throat, where I can smell her and feel the thump of her heart against my chest.

She disappears into the crowd, ponytail swinging, her whisky clutched in one hand. I turn back to Lucy, eyes wide and glaring, and she *laughs* at me. Spreads her hands in surrender.

"Sorry, Fraser. I wanted to nudge you two along."

"Mind your business next time," I growl, and Gideon curls an arm around her shoulders protectively. He shoots me a glare, but I'm not looking at him. I'm craning my neck, staring after Raine in the tangle of people.

"I am so confused," Beckett mutters. Keeley hushes him, amusement clear in the sound. This is a joke to them, but it's my life, my career, my *Raine.* Pushing into the crowd of strangers to find someone to flirt with. To test whether she's attracted to anyone else but me. *God,* I want to smash something.

I push to my feet, swiping my bottle off the table. And level Lucy with a look.

"This is not your doing. Don't get cocky."

She grins up at me. "Bye, Fraser."

I roll my eyes and push into the crowd, following the same direction as Raine. She's not tall enough for this, so damnably short, and that's another thing I need to lecture her over. If she's going to wander off in bars, she'd better wear a tall hat.

It takes far too long to spot her. My heart thunders faster and faster in my chest, my steps becoming more frantic as I search the shadowy corners. If she's found someone she wants to be alone with—fine. I won't interrupt, even though the thought sickens me. I'll go and rant uselessly at Beckett like a grown man.

But if she's bored or unhappy, or god forbid, *uncomfortable*, I'm snatching her back. This is a stupid experiment.

I find her in a shadowy alcove, leaning against a wall. My mouth runs dry at the sight, at the man looming over her, but the ringing in my ears starts to fade when I see her glazed expression. She nods and hums at the guy as he drones on and on, waving an arm around to illustrate whatever dull shit he's boring her with.

Thank god. Thank god. I push towards them.

This has gone on long enough.

9

Chapter Nine

God, this guy can talk. I picked him on a whim after wandering through the crowd, trying to find someone, *anyone*, who makes my blood pump faster like Fraser does. Who brings a flush to my cheeks and sends restless energy coursing under my skin.

It's a tall order. So obviously, I found no one. There are all the usual suspects, out at a bar near campus on a Wednesday night: rowdy sports teams; intense businessmen with their neckties pulled loose; flocks of grad students slumped over the booths, pale with exhaustion. And though objectively, I know that Lucy is right—there are plenty of textbook handsome guys in this bar—none of them hold my interest.

They're all predictable Same-y. Flat.

In the end, I let a guy pick me. He sidled up to me by the bar, offering to buy me another drink. So I agreed, and I let him tug me into this alcove to talk.

I've never made such a grave mistake.

If being dull were an Olympic sport, this guy would have a shot at the podium. He asked my name when he first approached me, then visibly forgot it, and hasn't asked me a question since. It's just a fountain of *words,* battering down on me—his classes, his career plans, his hobbies. That one time a guy in his dorm drew devil eyebrows on him in permanent marker. You know, really thrilling stuff.

I hum and nod, eyeing my exits, but if I go back to the booth too soon, Lucy will never let it drop. So I stand here and let Brent or Brock or whoever this is tell me his life story, as if I asked.

I feel Fraser approaching before I see him. My senses tingle somehow, my abdomen clenching tight, and then he's *here,* pushing through the noisy crowds. The stony expression on his face makes my thighs squeeze tight together.

I should thank Lucy, really. I should buy her chocolate.

Because if she hadn't meddled, with that mischievous glint in her doe eyes, I might never have seen *this* expression on Fraser's face. He's calm and collected to every one else, but I see the strain. I see the barely restrained hunger, the urgency to his steps.

He strides into the alcove, ignoring Brock-or-Brent completely, and takes me by the elbow.

"Enough. Let's go."

Part of me wants to push him further. Wants to see him *really* snap. And maybe if there weren't so much on the line, if his career weren't at risk, I'd do it. I'll drive him to madness with a smile on my face.

But Keeley's soft heart must be rubbing off on me, because I huff and let him pull me back towards the room.

"Hey, wait a second." Brock-or-Brent puts a hand on Fraser's arm. Fraser looks down at it, slow and deadly. The younger man whips his hand back, puffing up his chest to compensate.

"We're talking, dude."

"You're finished, *bro.*" Fraser spits the word like an insult. I can't believe this idiot is still pushing his luck—come on, it was hardly a great conversation—but he looks at me instead.

"Do you need help, um... Rachel? Is this man bothering you?"

I snort. It's a valiant attempt I guess, but it really took the shine off when he forgot my name. Plus this is a rescue I very much want, and I inch closer to Fraser in answer.

"I'm good. We know each other."

Brent-or-Brock drops it, grumbling under his breath as he pushes roughly past. Jeez, what a baby. Fraser clearly thinks so too, giving me a scathing look.

"That guy? Really?"

I shrug, enjoying his bitterness way too much. Hey, I've never thought of myself as a woman that men would fight over. And though that idiot barely counts as a rival, it is fascinating to watch the nerve leaping in Fraser's temple.

"Yeah. Sorry, Drummond. He seduced me with his stories about the lacrosse team."

Fraser uncoils a fraction. Finally realizes I'm teasing. But though he's eager to drag me back to the booth with our friends, I'm not so ready to end our time alone.

It's risky. Selfish. There are students in this bar. Probably college staff too. Anyone might recognize the both of us, and figure we're standing a little too close for professor and student.

Maybe it damns me to hell, but that just makes me flush hotter. I grab a fistful of Fraser's shirt and tug him back into the alcove.

"Just a few more minutes," I murmur as he crowds me back against the wall. From here, we're tucked away together, maybe only an elbow or a glimpse of shoulder showing.

"Raine," he says in warning, and I swear that's ninety percent of what he says to me. At least he knows my name. I yank him closer, sealing the length of his body against mine, relishing the solid heat of him. He's still dressed like a professor in gray pants and a white button down shirt, the first two buttons open at the collar.

It'll crease where I clutch him close. I like that.

"Call it research." I rise up on my toes, nipping at the underside of his jaw. "If it makes you feel better."

Because it's not research to me. Not anymore. I've drawn my conclusions: I want Fraser Drummond badly, like I've never wanted anyone before. And though maybe I could want someone else like this one day, if Fraser's an option... who cares?

"Nothing about this makes me feel better." His hands find my waist and squeeze, kneading the swell of my hips, and he shudders out a sigh before pressing a kiss onto my throat.

"Liar."

He hums, drawing a scorching trail along my skin, up to my chin, to my mouth. We both groan as his mouth crashes onto mine, his hips thrusting me back against the wall. He's everywhere, all around me, overwhelming and perfect, and how did I go since yesterday without experiencing this?

"Don't look for any more men." Fraser grinds the words out against my temple, both his hands buried in my hair. He's still rocking against me, rubbing the hard length of his cock against my hip. "You don't need them."

"Because I have you?"

He growls and flattens me harder against the wall. "Yes."

It's so base, so primal, and I freaking love it. I clutch him closer, fighting to feel every inch of him pressed against me. I don't even recognize myself like this—hazy and half out of my mind with lust.

"You've only kissed me once," I point out. "Then threw me out of your office two seconds later."

He has the decency to look aggrieved. He speaks to me between kisses, his mouth never more than a hair's breadth from mine.

"Don't bring up my flaws right now. There are too many to list, and we don't have time."

I nod, peering up at him. "You're right. I'll make you a list."

"Perfect. Send it to my email and I'll respond within five working days."

I laugh, breathless and giddy, and when he groans and steps back, my chest aches. I don't want to sneak around with him in the shadows. Okay—I do a bit. But I don't want him to retreat like this, regret and shame etched on his face.

"No." I smack his shoulder. "Don't do that. This was *good*. I liked it."

He tucks my hair behind my ear.

"So did I. But now it's time to go."

* * *

The rest of the evening crawls by. We go back to the booth, cheeks flushed, and slide into the seats, both ignoring the meaningful glances thrown our way.

Lucy smiles at me nervously, and I shoot her a smirk. She softens, relieved, and I sip at my drink. Conversation rises again, on some neutral, harmless topic, and I let it wash over me.

It's not fair. I want to cuddle up to Fraser like the others. They're all so relaxed and unashamed, safe in the knowledge that their relationships are no one else's business.

Could we have that? I peer up at Fraser, but he's back to not meeting my eye. Staring at the table, his jaw rigid.

No. Fraser doesn't seem like the straightforward type. He's in a job he clearly hates, after all, and god knows why. He moved to another country and barely speaks about his family.

Professor Fraser Drummond is kind of a mess. Not the sort of man to make a healthy decision, weighing the pros and cons before making a choice. It was easier in some ways, for Gideon and Beckett. A simple calculation—the loves of their lives before their careers.

With Fraser, it would surely be a scandal. A huge fallout, with the two of us left dazed in the crater.

I grab my glass and take another sip, hissing at it burns my throat.

"Are you okay?" Lucy asks as we walk back to the apartment together. Beckett is here, though Gideon and Fraser have both gone home. He's been spending less and less time on the coast as his schedule opens up, which means more and more Beckett in our apartment.

Maybe it's good we're all moving out. It could get pretty crowded, all jumbled in together. Especially with those shoulders.

I nudge her with my elbow, my hands shoved in my pockets. The evening is still light, airy and floral, and I suck down big lungfuls.

"Yep. I'm good."

"I'm sorry if I pushed you too hard—"

"Pushed Fraser too hard, more like." Lucy huffs a laugh, her tiny legs working double time to keep up as our footsteps echo along the sidewalk.

"You didn't mind, though, right?"

I chew that over. It'll hurt more now, not to have him. That's for sure. But do I regret it?

"No. I didn't mind." I scuff my sneaker on the paving stones. "But… don't get your hopes up. Okay, Luce?"

"What do you mean?" God, her eyes get big when she's sad. Gideon doesn't stand a chance.

"I mean he's not like Gideon. Or Beckett. Fraser doesn't know what the hell he wants. He's not going to give everything up in a big romantic gesture. He's going to…" I trail off, swallowing hard. "He'll back himself into a corner, then things will explode. And he'll resent me for it. Even if he doesn't mean to."

"You don't know that," Lucy whispers. "It might not go that way."

I think of Fraser's tetchy manner whenever he's in the Wellness Center. The lost, angry look on his face when he fell asleep at the talk.

"It will."

Lucy sighs like the world is weighing on her tiny shoulders. And she hums when I sling my arm around her, tugging her close.

"It'll be alright, Lucy. Mommy and Daddy will still love you."

She hiccups a laugh. "But where will I spend Christmas?"

"We'll keep you in a box, exactly halfway between our apartments."

She squeezes me in a hug. "That sounds nice."

I have a sneaking suspicion that she's only here tonight because of me. Most nights, she stays with Gideon—whether at his place or ours. For her to send him away and walk home beside me… she's worried.

Damn. Am I that transparent?

10

Chapter Ten

I loiter in the quad as the evening light draws in, a takeout coffee clutched in both hands. I've got the shifty feeling that everyone must be looking at me, reading my misdeeds on my face, but in reality no one spares me a glance. Students file past, hurrying on their own with arms full of books, or in pairs and small groups, walking slower and chatting. Pigeons peck at the day's dropped crumbs on the paving stones, and tired administrators spill out of the department offices and trudge towards the staff parking lot.

She's late. It's six minutes past six. Does that mean her enthusiasm is wearing off? Or did I tease her too much for coming to my office five minutes early that day?

Classic, really. I've played myself.

When Raine finally careens around the corner of the library, her black jacket collar rucked up on one side, I blow out a breath.

"What time do you call this?" I lift my wrist to show her my watch. Raine grins and swipes the coffee from my hand.

"Sorry. Got caught up shelving."

"A true emergency, then."

She lifts one shoulder. "We can't all ditch our jobs when we get bored of them." There's something behind her studiously casual words. Not judgement, exactly, but *something*. A hint. Layered meaning. It makes my hackles rise, especially after she turned up late.

Raine says what she means. That's why she's so refreshing.

"Let's get on then. The talk already started." If she can hear my bitter tone, she doesn't say anything. And how did we suddenly get here—talking around each other in circles? Only two days ago, I kissed her up against a bar wall.

The awkwardness between us intensifies as we push through the Psychology Department doors and stride through the corridors in silence. Raine knows the way now, but she makes no mention of the increasing shabbiness this time. Nor does she tease me about falling asleep the last time we were here. All the easy lightness I've missed, that I've been craving every minute without her—it's gone.

We might as well be student and professor again.

The projection booth is as we left it last time. I walk straight over to the chairs and drag them by the glass, setting them closer together tonight. When Raine comes to join me, she's smiling. *Really* smiling.

The knot in my chest loosens slightly.

Okay. Okay. A bit of weirdness is normal. Hell, it's normal when a regular couple starts to date, let alone a pairing that could end in scandal. We're starting off disadvantaged, with two massive suitcases of metaphorical baggage before we've even begun. So I tell myself to get out of my own head as Raine drops into one of the chairs.

She peers through the glass, at the bustling lecture hall below us. It's always surreal being here. Like some kind of reverse fish bowl. We can see them but they can't see us, and the buzz of conversation drifting through the glass is warped.

"What's the topic tonight?" she asks.

"I don't know." When she spins and stares at me, I'm smirking. "I have another sort of lesson in mind."

It takes a second, but I see the exact moment Raine catches my meaning. Her chest rises quicker, her breaths coming faster, and a flush darkens her cheeks.

She licks her bottom lip. The flash of her pink tongue makes my pulse skitter. "Alright, professor. What am I learning tonight?"

I don't answer her right away. The moment we're spinning here is still fragile. Still tainted with awkwardness. So I prowl around her instead, dropping to my knees in front of her chair, my back to the tinted glass.

"You liked what we did in the bar." It's not a question. This, at least, I'm sure of. I can still hear her whimpers, muffled by our kiss.

"Yes." Raine watches me wide-eyed, her fingers picking nervously at the seams of her jeans. Our faces our level, and her gaze keeps dropping to my mouth.

"What did you like about it?"

Raine swallows. "All of it."

Warmth spreads through my chest, shimmering and golden. But I push that away, because that's not what this is about. This is an education, of sorts.

"Give me specifics, Raine."

"I liked the…" She clears her throat and starts again. "I liked when you pressed me against the wall. Feeling, um. Feeling all of you."

"Good." I slide my palms up her thighs, bare beneath her cut off shorts. Goosebumps ripple in my wake. "Very good. What else?"

"I liked kissing you." She's bolder now. Her mouth quirks in challenge. "And I liked that you were so jealous."

I can't deny it. I was ready to rip the furniture apart. Not-not *really*, I'm not a complete animal, but the urge was there alright. Urgent and vicious under my skin.

"Would you like to hear my theory?" My fingertips trace along the hem of her shorts. Raine's breath hitches, and she squirms to give me better access.

"I guess. You're making a big enough deal out of it."

"It's worth it."

"Go on, then."

I grin, tucking one knuckle under her shorts. I drag it back and forth, back and forth, over her gorgeous brown skin. The air in here is stuffy and stale, all the furniture caked with dust, but right now I wouldn't trade this room for a breezy meadow.

"Here's my theory." Raine's lips part as I talk, her eyes fixed on mine. Rapt. "You didn't just like what we did. You liked *where* we did it. You liked the risk of getting caught. Of being seen."

Her chest heaves, that damn pink-wigged skull lurching around on her lapel. I'm right. I'm so fucking right. I've got Raine Laghari's number, I *know* what she wants, and I'm going to be the man to give it to her.

"Tell me I'm right," I murmur. I'm pushing my luck by making her lay it all out like this, but she needs to be clear. She needs to be all-in, or we'll just sit and watch the talk like last time.

Well, mostly like last time. Hopefully I'll stay awake like a functioning adult.

"I…" Raine's cheeks are flushed. Her eyes dart to the side and back again. Then she tosses up her hands, sitting back in the chair. "I don't know! I never do this stuff. How am I supposed to *know*?"

"You're a clever girl." I reach out and twiddle a lock of her hair. Wind it round and around my knuckle. "Consider your reactions, then and now. And make an educated guess."

"And if I say you're wrong?" Raine lifts her chin in challenge. I stifle a laugh.

"Then I'm wrong. Only you can decide what you want."

She looks oddly disappointed at that statement. Like she wanted me to challenge her, to tease her further, and I file *that* away for future reference. If Raine wants me to be cruel with her, to set her blood pumping with ruthlessness… I'm more than happy to oblige. But tonight isn't about that.

Baby steps. One illicit fantasy at a time.

Raine chews on the inside of her cheek, reaching out to card her fingers through my hair while she thinks it over. It's such a casually intimate gesture—and look at me, I'm doing the same fucking thing. We stowed away in here, petting each other, and how is it that we keep risking everything to *cuddle*?

"Raine." She blinks and comes back to herself.

"Yes." She gives a small nod. "Whatever you're offering, I want that."

It's an intriguing carte blanche, but there is a set plan in motion here. Since it occurred to me last night as I lay awake at 3am, I haven't been able to get the image out of my head: Raine sat in this chair, her hands white-knuckled on the arm rests and her legs tossed over my shoulders as I bury my head between her thighs.

"Alright." My mouth tugs up in a smile. "Sit back, Raine. And try to relax."

* * *

She's every bit as intoxicating as I imagined.

The stolen kisses we've already shared—those should have warned me. Should have set those faulty alarm bells ringing in my mind. But instead, I got a taste—not enough, *never* enough—and got cocky. Got caught up on the idea of showing off, of fulfilling her secret desires, and imprinting myself on her brain in the process.

It's a trap. A trap I laid for myself. This isn't going to be Raine's downfall at all, not when she's making those tiny, breathy noises that will surely play on a loop in my head until death.

Not when she's so fucking responsive, squirming in her chair, her hips bucking up to press harder against my mouth. Raine grips the armrests just like I'd pictured, and when I glance up from between her thighs, she's staring glassy-eyed out at the lecture hall.

She's dazed. So turned on that it's knocked the breath out of her, and I'd be smug if I weren't just as bad. I lick at her like an animal, messy and uncontrolled, with none of the finesse I'd planned for. She's *ruined* me, and I groan against her slick pussy, plunging my tongue as deep as it will go. Raine yelps, her hips lifting off the seat, and a man a few seats over in the back row of the lecture hall peers over his shoulder. He squints at the tinted glass, at most seeing shadows, then turns back to the talk. I watch him out of the corner of my eye, never letting up, never giving her respite.

Raine whimpers. A bead of sweat runs down the back of her thigh.

76

I love her like this. She's naturally straightforward anyway, but when it comes to her pleasure, Raine keeps no secrets. She's gloriously unabashed. And when she grips a handful of my hair, yanking until my eyes tear, I swat the side of her ass loud enough that the speaker pauses.

"Sh!" Raine's grinning, eyes screwing shut as her head rolls back. I nip her sensitive inner thigh and bury my face back between her legs, never mind my aching jaw and tongue.

This is the only work out I care about. Licking Raine until she forgets everything. Everyone but me.

"Fraser. Shit. Fraser."

"'S mphrofessr," I say, muffled against her pussy.

"Shut up." She's laughing silently, her breath hitching as she moans. "Oh my god, please shut up."

I won't shut up. What I *will* do is slide my middle finger into her entrance. I go slowly, crooking it to stroke against her inner walls, and then she's coming, clamping down on me like a vice.

She stiffens in the chair, rigid and trembling, as wave after wave of sensation rocks her frame. I desperately want to sit back and watch her properly, but more than that, I want to draw this out. To wring every last whimper from those lips. And when she finally slumps in the seat, batting me away clumsily, I sit back on my heels and wipe my mouth, chest heaving.

Fuck. *Fuck.*

Please, lord that I do not believe in. Let that have wrecked her as much as it did me.

"Oh my god." Raine's words are slurred. Her legs are still slung over my shoulders, heavier now that she's so relaxed. I place her feet gently on the floor, fishing around for the little heap of her shorts and panties.

"Leave it." She cracks an eye, watching me lazily. "I'll get them in a minute." An imperious hand reaches for me. "It's your turn."

I can't hide my snort, and she straightens, offended. Both her eyes blink open, and she takes in my grin with outright scorn.

"What's so funny?"

"You are." I flick her kneecap. "Admit it, Raine. You're boneless. You can barely sit up in your chair."

"I will recover any second," she begins hotly, but I lunge forward and kiss her. She huffs but kisses me back, her nails scratching at my jaw line.

"Let me have this." We break apart for breath, and I murmur the words between kisses. "Let me be unbearably smug. Just for a moment."

It's Raine's turn to snort. "Wow. For a moment? It's like you've never met yourself." She pulls back and frowns over my shoulder. "I wonder what the talk was about."

"Raine. Don't ruin this for me."

We're still grinning and bickering twenty minutes later when we spill out of the projection booth into the corridor. Raine's hair is wild, and mine is probably worse. We're both rumpled and flushed, laughing and standing too close to each other.

"Drummond?"

I freeze, horror sliding icy cold down my spine. Time slows as I turn, my grin morphing into a grimace, and find the head of the department standing part way down the corridor. He's stepping out of an office, a stack of books balanced on one forearm, and his expression is grim as he looks between us.

"Who is this?"

11

Chapter Eleven

The old professor looks appalled. He glances between the two of us, measuring the distance between us; our relaxed postures; the matching disarray of our clothes. Fraser is rigid, the color draining from his cheeks, so I take over. I inch away from him casually, putting space between us, and call out to the other man in a bright voice.

Nothing to see here. No reason to suspect. Guilty people don't chat, right, professor?

"Hi, sir!" Old men love being called 'sir'. "I'm Raine. Professor Drummond's girlfriend." Fraser turns to me, visibly horrified, so I keep talking before he ruins this. "I'm visiting for the week from home. In…" I wrack my brain quickly. "L.A."

The old guy visibly relaxes. He goes from scandalized to just plain irritated. I guess Fraser can still get in trouble for screwing around on campus, but at least I'm not a *student*. Right?

Fraser is deathly silent. I elbow him and he jerks back to life, wrapping a tense arm around my shoulders.

"Yes. My apologies, Graham. Raine here wanted to see where I worked."

The professor grumbles something, shaking his head. Then, fixing Fraser with a glare, he says: "We will discuss this tomorrow."

It's a dismissal. No, it's a freaking miracle is what it is, but Fraser is rigid as he hustles me away. His jaw is locked tight, his back ramrod straight, and fury rolls off him in waves. I let him march me down the corridor in thrumming silence, our footsteps clattering in the stairwells, and only once we've spilled out of the back exit to the parking lot does he round on me, eyes sparking.

"What the fuck was that? What were you *thinking?*"

I cross my arms and stand my ground. "I was thinking someone had to save your ass."

He rakes a hand through his hair. It was already a mess from me tugging on it, from everything we just did, but now he's rumpled for a different reason. I freaking *hate* that. Resentment simmers in me at the sight, and my mouth pinches in a firm line as he rants.

"You're a student here, Raine. In this fucking department! Do you know how fast gossip about the staff travels? Don't you think any of your teachers might hear the description of Raine, my girlfriend from L.A. and put two and two together?"

He cuts off with a groan, digging the heels of his palms into his eyes. When he lowers them, he looks so freaking miserable that suddenly all I want to do is go to him. I step forward, arms outstretched, but he reels back like I'm poisonous.

"Raine! Jesus Christ. Haven't you caused me enough trouble for one night?"

My arms drop. *Trouble?* Haven't *I* caused enough trouble? My heart pounds so hard, I feel it in my teeth. A bruise spreads through my gut, and I wheeze like I'm wounded from an impact.

I drag in a slow breath through my nose, and when I talk, my voice is quiet. Hard and empty.

"My apologies, professor." Fraser flinches, but I keep going. He's earned this—every last word. "You kissed me in the bar. You invited me tonight. You initiated everything we did. And *you* wanted to play with the risk of getting caught."

His face falls as I speak, and his hand twitches towards me. I watch it, but he doesn't make the move. Doesn't try to make this right. And suddenly, I am so freaking tired of Fraser Drummond.

"You know what?" I smile at him, but it's warped. Vicious. "I'm done. Experiment over."

My shoes scuff over the parking lot tarmac as I walk away, arms stiff at my sides. The evening is darkening, indigo patches of clouds warning rain, and the shadowed tree branches claw at the sky. But even though the only sound is my ragged breathing, the *thud thud thud* of my heart, Fraser doesn't say anything. Doesn't call after me. Doesn't even say he's freaking sorry.

But what did I expect? I told Lucy it would go this way.

Sometimes it sucks to always be right.

* * *

The apartment door slams open, bouncing off the wall. Tiny flecks of paint skitter onto the floorboards.

"Shit." I drop my backpack with a thump. "I'll pay for that."

"What's wrong?" Lucy's wide-eyed on the sofa, her little head poking up over the cushions. Keeley's wedged in beside her, her lilac hair scraped into a topknot. The TV's on, some nineties rom com playing at a low volume, and the tang of nail polish is sharp in the air.

Girls' night. Perfect.

"What's wrong?" I muse aloud as I trudge toward the sofa, rolling my head on my stiff neck. I've been rigid with anger for the whole walk home. Rigor mortis is setting in. "What's wrong... I would say that Professor Fraser Drummond is *wrong*. So freaking wrong he doesn't know his head from his ass."

"Ah." Keeley spins around and rummages beside her. When she turns back, she offers up a crumpled bag of toffees.

"No thanks." I flop down next to Lucy. Those toffees are lethal. If I chew them in anger, I'll probably rip out my teeth.

"It was nearly so neat." I hold up my hands in a picture frame shape. "Three of them. Three of us. No outcasts."

"You're not an outcast!" Lucy is horrified. Pink spots glow on her cheeks. "You never could be. That's—that wasn't why you were dating him, was it?"

I sink lower into the cushions. "No. It wasn't." It wouldn't hurt so freaking much if it was. There's an ache in my chest that won't go away. And just thinking about why I did get involved with him—his sardonic smile, his dry humor, the way he kissed me with his whole body, holding nothing back—I suck in a shaky breath.

It's fine. It's fine.

It was just an experiment. And now it's over.

"We got caught in the department." I sound numb. Exhausted. "He freaked out after. Said I'd caused him too much trouble."

Keeley lets out a hiss. Human-ball-of-sunshine Keeley never gets pissed off, so the disgusted look she gives me is like balm to my soul.

"That asshole. You're too good for him, Raine."

I grunt and snuggle into Lucy's shoulder. I don't want to talk about this any more. I want a cheesy rom com and Keeley's righteous ire and, once my jaw has unclenched, about a dozen of those toffees.

Fraser Drummond is nothing. A bump in the road.

And I'll keep telling myself so until I believe it.

* * *

I wait until the others are asleep. Until the apartment is cloaked in shadows and moonlight filters through the windows. The living room is silent, the TV screen crackling with static, and the sofa is littered with scratchy, balled up toffee wrappers.

I want to know. Want to conduct another quick experiment. I need to see how badly Fraser has taken over my insides.

I push off the sofa, scooping up my laptop and wandering into my bedroom. The walls are dotted with polaroids, taken during my photography phase, and my sewing machine hunches on my cluttered desk. I don't spend much time in here—it's the smallest room, and kind of cramped.

I guess my next place might be nicer.

It's a hollow comfort. The whole point of this apartment is the girls sleeping in their rooms. The family we've built together. It doesn't matter if my next bedroom has a four-poster and an ensuite—it won't be the same.

"Lighten up, Laghari," I mutter to myself, pushing the door shut behind me. My socked feet scuff over the rug as I cross to the bed, lowering the laptop onto the covers.

I change first. Slide into an old pair of jersey shorts and a band t-shirt. Tug out my hair tie, finger-combing my waves and massaging my throbbing temples.

I'll try quickly. An information gathering mission. And if Fraser ruins this for me, I'll… Well, I'll hate him more than I already do. I climb into bed and stare at the laptop, chewing the inside of my cheek. Then I huff and snap it closed, placing it on a nearby chair.

I don't want those sites. Videos of strangers going at it. I'm sure they can be fun, but not... not now.

I close my eyes and shuffle down in the bed. Smooth a palm over the soft skin of my stomach.

Trying to touch myself without thinking of Fraser is like telling someone not to think of elephants. Every place my fingers delve, he's been there already. Shown me how good it can feel. And when I try daydreaming, try to imagine another man, another place, his face keeps reappearing in my mind's eye.

"You don't need another man," he growls into my ear, just like he did in the bar.

"Because I have you?"

"Yes."

I huff and yank my hands away. If I have to picture Fraser, I'm not doing it. That's like letting him win. So I roll over instead, mashing my cheek into the pillow, and try to ignore the hot pulsing between my legs. It's fierce and insistent, a flush breaking over my skin, but I grind my teeth and wedge my palms between my knees.

I force myself to remember the other things he said.

"What the fuck was that? What were you thinking?"

"Haven't you caused me enough trouble for one night?"

Asshole. Cruel, clueless asshole. I sniffle, burying my chin in the covers.

Good riddance. The results of the experiment are clear: Fraser Drummond will break my heart.

12

Chapter Twelve

I know I've fucked up the second Raine turns around and walks away. Her thick ponytail swings behind her, heavy with glossy waves, and my pulse thuds so hard I can hear it in my ears. She strides down the path, her head held tall, and even leaving me like this, she's magnificent.

How can I call back a woman like that? After what I've done to her—the things I've said?

Fuck.

Besides, it's not like anything has changed in the last two minutes. I'm still a professor and she is a student; this was never going to be a long term thing. My job won't allow it.

I scrub both hands over my face, groaning loudly enough to startle the pigeons. A cold breeze rustles the trees, gusting under my collar, and suddenly the thought of going home like this, alone and angry, is too depressing to contemplate. I can't go from the warmth and technicolor of Raine Laghari to my silent, gloomy apartment. I can't.

I dig my phone out of my pocket as I walk, striding in the opposite direction. The head of the department; the fallout;

this bleeding hole in my chest—I'll deal with it all tomorrow.

"Where are you?" I grind out as soon as Gideon picks up.

"At home. Working. Why?"

"Meet me in Donovan's in twenty minutes."

"You know, these distress calls could use more warning—"

"Please, Gid." I let some of my desperation bleed through, and he quiets.

"Okay. Okay. I'll be there soon."

I've never been one for sending out an S.O.S. For needing company to drown my sorrows, or a sympathetic ear to lay my troubles on. I've always dealt with things the Drummond family way—by burying them deep down inside and throwing away the key.

I don't need to read my own guidance counselor leaflets to know that's unhealthy bullshit. But it's not easy breaking the habits of a lifetime.

Maybe this is a good thing. I'm reaching out. Sharing my troubles. Seeking advice, as long as it doesn't come attached to too much judgement.

Yeah, right. I just don't want to be alone with my thoughts.

* * *

Gideon gets there before me. He has a bottle of beer waiting for me on the bar countertop, and a wry smile tugging his mouth. That amusement drains away when he gets a good look at me.

I must be a state.

"Thanks for coming," I say gruffly, taking the offered beer. Now that we're both here and I have to act like a human, I'm regretting everything. Stewing alone in my apartment doesn't sound so bad.

"Any time," Gideon says slowly, watching me with a slight frown. "Is this about Raine by any chance?"

I startle, almost choking on my beer, but why is that surprising? I've been bloody obvious enough. I stalked after her through the crowd in this exact bar, kissing the breath from her lungs in an alcove.

God, I've been so reckless. So eager to risk everything. Raine is right—this is all my own doing.

I can't believe I said those things to her. I knock back the beer, taking an angry swig. Gideon watches everything, a bemused expression on his face.

I guess this seems simple to him. He managed it well enough after all—when the time came, he made the right choices with Lucy. Eventually.

"Tell me what happened." He raises a palm as I roll my eyes. "Don't be a dick. Just tell me what happened."

Alright then.

"I got caught with her. By the head of the department. Then straight after, I said... some things. Some awful fucking things, really, and she's done. Which is—well. Who can blame her?"

"Okay." Gideon rubs his eyebrow. "I need more context. Are we commiserating the damage to your career? Or that she's gone?"

I open my mouth to say *my career, obviously,* since it's been years of my life and my biggest achievement. All those painful years of hard work and drudgery. All those constant doubts about whether I was even in the right field. I gave up so much for this career—my home, the closeness of my family, a dating life, my *sanity*—that of course that's what we're commiserating.

Right?

I take another swig, unconvinced. Gideon cracks another

smile, shaking his head as he leans back against the bar.

"No rush, man. I'll let you get there on your own."

"What the hell have I been doing?" I ask hoarsely. "How did I make such a mess of things? For *years?*"

Gideon shrugs. "Success is heady. Addictive. You're good at what you do. And let's face it—you've never really got the hang of being happy."

That's a hell of a thing to say to someone, and he braces like I'm going to ream him out. But he's right.

God. I'm a wreck.

"I've fucked up." His mouth twists in sympathy as the weight of what I've done comes tumbling down. "I've scared her off over nothing. What the hell do I do?"

"Unscare her?" He spreads his hands in surrender. "Sorry, man. You're the one who knows her best."

Is that true? A pang of fierce longing rattles through me. I hope it's true. I can certainly read her moods from the set of her mouth. The tone of her voice. The way she plays with the ends of her hair. I can tell when she's thoughtful or in analysis-mode. And I can tell when all that has fallen away, and she's enraptured. Swallowed whole by the moment, her eyes bright and her lips parting.

"Okay. Damn it. Okay." I pick up my beer. I put it back down. I'm a professor, for god's sake. Why can I suddenly not think straight?

Because for the first time in years, this matters.

That's why.

* * *

The department head calls me into his office first thing in the morning. I'm expecting the email—I've been on campus since dawn, my office in the Wellness Center strewn with cardboard boxes. I already packed up my abandoned office back in the department. How did I accumulate so much crap over the last few years?

My phone pings from the windowsill. I swipe it up eagerly, hoping for something from Raine—hell, even hate mail—but it's Graham. His summons is quick and terse.

Not my biggest fan, then.

Just last night, that might have spun me out. Before speaking to Gideon, before finally getting some clarity, this meeting would have filled me with dread. But this morning, I hum and tap out a quick reply.

I'll be there. It's one more job to tick off the list.

Here's my thinking: Raine does not put up with assholes. To her credit, she has barely any patience for jerks. I've managed to land myself squarely in that box, so if I want any chance at all with her, I need to put things right first. Show her that I can actually make a decision; that I don't have to be an irredeemable mess.

It's a humbling mission. And one I'm not sure I'd go on, if it weren't for Raine.

Raine. I haven't stopped thinking about her. Obsessing and stewing and pining like a schoolboy. It's fine. In this, at least, dignity is overrated.

"You sent for me?" I poke my head around Graham's office door ten minutes later. He startles from behind his desk, apparently surprised that I'm already on campus. The department head's office suffers from the same delusions of grandeur as the lobby: every surface is burnished brass or rich mahogany. Graham himself is underwhelmed by his furniture—a drab, self-important man in a baggy white shirt and smudged spectacles.

There's a white tuft of tissue stuck under his ear. Must have nicked himself shaving this morning.

Despite his grooming injury, Graham rallies quickly and clears his throat. He ushers me inside, gesturing to the visitor's chair opposite his desk—noticeably a few inches lower than normal.

When I sit down, we're still eye level. That shouldn't please me so much.

"You know why you're here, Drummond."

I lean back and smile. "Remind me."

He bristles and I stifle a laugh. I shouldn't enjoy this, shouldn't torment the poor man, but the truth is I've been longing for this day. Dreaming of leaving this half life behind for so long that I forgot what it feels like to actually enjoy something.

"Is this amusing to you?" He sucks his teeth, trimmed mustache shifting. "We take the conduct of our staff very seriously in this department."

"That's good." I nod. "It's good to have standards."

Graham blinks. "Yes. Right."

I'm throwing him off, derailing him, and that's not actually why I'm here. I rein it in, prompting him to keep talking.

"It was poor judgement on my part, to bring Raine here after hours."

"Yes." He gathers steam again. "Yes, exactly. I cannot let such a misstep go unpunished."

"Nor should you." I take a moment to peer around the office shelves. Graham has rows of impressive looking leather hardbacks, but it's the potted plant that I notice. Its leaves are drooping. "You should water that plant," I say suddenly. "It's thirsty. See?"

"Professor Drummond." Graham breathes heavily, the row of buttons on his shirt rising and falling behind the desk. "Your conduct last night was bad enough, but your attitude this morning—"

"I quit." This is taking far too long. And the sight of that plant sent pain rippling through my chest. *Raine.* "I'll serve my notice if you like. But you should know that Raine is a student here."

Graham splutters, his cheeks flushing red.

"I'll take that as a no. I'm just packing up my office now, actually, and I'll be off campus within the hour."

"Good," Graham manages, tugging at his collar. "That's—yes. You'd better leave."

"Bye, then." I feel ten pounds lighter as I launch to my feet. "Don't forget the plant."

My footsteps drum on the floorboards as I cross to the door. Time to get out here. Time to move on.

13

Chapter Thirteen

On days like these, I'm weirdly grateful for how boring my library job is. I can fall into a rhythm—pick up book, put on shelf, pull cart—and my brain can leave the building.

I don't want to think. Not right now. Not while I can't trust my brain not to circle back to *him.* I want to shelve these books and drag my squeaky cart, and earn a wage so I can afford a decent studio after the summer.

The library is blessedly quiet this afternoon. Pale spring sunshine has filled the quad, and all the students are rushing outside with their laptops and library books to study in its glow. It's a sign of the changing seasons, more undeniable evidence that graduation and summer are coming, and the big wide world is yawning open to swallow us whole.

Keeley and Lucy have it figured out. I will too. I'm good at this stuff—adapting. Rolling with the punches. Lucy sat up late with me last night setting up an online shop for my embroidery designs. And when I woke up this morning, I'd received my first order—twelve whole dollars for an octopus pattern I created last year.

It may not be millions, but it's a start. It's money *I* earned, with one of my designs, and it's the first hint of something I could do after college.

Maybe full time. Maybe as a side thing. I don't know everything yet, but I'll figure it out. That's what I try to focus on when my book-shelving fugue breaks now and then. My embroidery. Not the poor bruised organ in my chest.

"Excuse me." I drag my cart along, the wheel squeaking. No one talks to me in the library. There are librarians for that. "I need help to find a book, please."

"Try the desks—" I cut off as I turn. Fraser stands behind me, hands in his pockets. He looks… different than yesterday. Lighter. Happier. God, I hate him for that.

"What do you want?" I say flatly. No cutesy role play this time. I've had about enough of his bullshit as I can handle.

"You." That word thuds through my brain. He says it with conviction. Like his mind is made up and no force on this planet could sway him away. "I quit my job, Raine."

I lick my lips, mind racing. The hardback I'm clutching trembles in my hand.

"You got fired? Because of me?"

He smirks and steps closer. My heart pounds faster and faster, my breaths coming quick. But that can't be right, because if that was true he'd be furious. Lashing out like yesterday.

"No. I quit. By choice."

"I don't…" His gaze roves hungrily over me. Over my rumpled t-shirt and holey jeans. I couldn't be bothered to try and look good this morning, but he doesn't seem to even notice. He looks *starved* for me. "I don't understand, professor."

"Not a professor anymore." He steps closer again. My back

93

hits the shelves, the hardback in my hand slipping back onto the cart. "Not anything. So I'd like to propose another experiment."

I should tell him to back off. To stop crowding me, blocking out the lights with those freaking shoulders, but I don't. I bite my lip and wish he'd come closer. Breach this distance between us. *Traitorous heart.*

"What kind of experiment?"

"To see whether you can forgive me. Whether you still want me when I'm not a professor." A hint of uncertainty creeps into his eyes. "To see if you'll let me fix this."

I force the words out. "And how would you do that?" My hands ball at my sides. I press my fists to the shelves to keep from reaching for him.

"I'd tell you I'm sorry." He lifts his hands, achingly slowly. Slow enough that I could move away. Could tell him to stop. I don't. They come to rest on my waist, feather light through my t-shirt. "I'd tell you how miraculous you are. How my world dims when you're gone."

My laugh is strangled. "It's been less than twenty four hours."

"So?" Fraser grins, closing the distance between us. His chest brushes against my front. "Some results are really fucking obvious straight away." He takes a deep breath. "I messed up, Raine. Please let me fix it. Whatever you need, however you want me to do it—I'll do it."

I chew on my lip, pretending to think. His warmth is bleeding through my t-shirt, tickling over my skin. I can smell him and feel him, and god, practically taste him already.

He's an idiot. *My* idiot. And I've missed him so much.

"There needs to be more groveling."

His eyes twinkle. "I can do that."

"And a cappucino."

"Done."

"And I want—um. Oh, I know. I want to read your research."

He tuts, bending his head to drag his lips over my jaw. "Raine, love." His words flutter the hairs by my ear. "Haven't you suffered enough?"

* * *

Any college campus library definitely has a rich history of secret hookups. The quarterback and the nerdy bookworm. The librarian and the janitor. Two rival professors, banging all their academic fury out between the hidden, untraveled stacks. Maybe it's the geek in me, but I've always thought libraries are really freaking horny.

It helps to be a library worker. One of the re-shelving elves. Because I know all the secret spots; the private nooks and crannies. I know where to take Fraser's hand and drag him into the shadows.

"The Classics section? Very kinky."

"Shut up." He's grinning as I tug him down by the shirt, sealing our mouths in a kiss. This floor is empty, thank god—there are no dry coughs or turning pages—but we still have to be quiet. Heat pools in my core at the thought.

Or maybe it's Fraser's hands, roaming hot and eager over me. Gripping my hips; squeezing my waist; kneading my shoulders. Fraser touches me like he's committing me to memory. Like he's not convinced yet that we're okay, that this will happen again.

Well, that's no good. And I have the solution. I grab his shirt and swing him around, shoving him up against the shelves. The little *oof* noise he makes is music to my ears, and when I drop to my knees, he curses and plunges his hands into my hair. My hair tie patters to the carpet beside me.

I pause, reaching for his button.

"Don't get this mixed up, okay? This is not a reward for shitty behavior."

Fraser places one solemn hand on his heart. "I promise not to think I deserve this—"

He cuts off with a hiss as I wrench his pants open, slipping my hand through the gap in the fabric to grip his cock. He's hot and steely in my palm; so hard it must surely hurt. And when I draw him out, glancing around the empty stacks before giving an exploratory tug—his left knee jerks, almost buckling, and *this* is what power feels like. My sarcastic professor, mussed and at my mercy, scrabbling for purchase against the shelves. Groaning as I take him in my mouth. Hips thrusting like he just can't help it.

"Fuck. *Raine.* Oh god. That fucking mouth."

So he's kind of a dirty talker. That's no plot twist. Fraser Drummond has that *look* about him, filthy and knowing and game, and god I'm glad to finally put him through his paces. I show this asshole no mercy, bobbing my head and hollowing my cheeks and taking him almost all the way into my throat. The soft patter of curses falling on my shoulders—it only eggs me on. Only makes me suck harder; swirl my tongue; scratch my nails down his thighs.

"You're such an asshole," I gasp as I come up for breath, resting my forehead against his hip. His fingers card gently through my hair. "Never do that shit to me again."

"I won't." He plucks at my shoulder. "Raine. Love. Come up here."

The room tilts as I stagger upright, lightheaded and scraped hollow. Fraser takes one look at me and gathers me into his arms, pressing kisses on my hair and murmuring sweet nothings.

I bat him off. We're not done here. He can dote on me when we're done. Once I finally, *finally*, get Professor F. Drummond inside me.

"Do you have a condom?" My voice is muffled by his shirt.

"Ah." I pull back to look at him. He has the grace to sound abashed. "Yes, actually. Not because I assumed anything, but, you know. Hope springs eternal."

I stifle a smile, turning to peer through the gap in the stacks. He leans with me, keeping his arms wrapped tight, and I strain to listen for students. There's no scratch of pens. No tapping of keys.

I bite my lip and turn back to him. "Time for one last study, Drummond?"

He's gentler than I imagined. To begin with, anyway. He spins me around and presses me back against the stacks, covering my body from head to toe. He kisses me like I'm precious. Like he can't believe his luck. And my heart throbs so hard in my chest that it's just this side of pain, and my head spins, and it's almost too much, but then he nips my bottom lip. His teeth are sharp, unforgiving, and *this* is the Fraser I know. The one I've touched myself thinking about.

He's demanding. Harsh. Rough with his movements; possessive and firm. He slams me back against the stacks, never mind that the shelves dig into my back, and he plunges his tongue into my mouth.

"*Yes,*" I hiss when he breaks away, scorching a trail of lips and teeth down my throat. He pushes one hand inside my t-shirt, kneading my breast inside my bra, and that's almost cruel too.

Heat pulses between my legs where his sculpted thighs thrust against me.

"You want to get fucked in the library, Raine?" Yeah, here's the talker. He spins me around and presses my front into the shelves, swatting my ass through my worn jeans. "I'll give you something to think about, love. Something for your research."

"So freaking smug," I mumble, already hazy from his touch. He takes over, reaching around and flicking my jeans open, then drags them down my legs in one swift motion. He kicks my feet wider. Steps up to my back.

"Are you sure?" he asks, voice ragged, hands roaming over my hips. His fingers play beneath the hem of my underwear.

"Shut up," I moan, my ass thrusting against him. Dignity? What dignity? "Yes, I'm sure."

He touches me first, for all his urgency. Traces his broad fingertips up and down my slit, then dips into my entrance and works me open. He swirls the pad of his thumb over my clit, and I moan loud and reckless as I drop my head forwards.

"Fraser. I swear to god. Don't make me fucking come back there."

"Yes, ma'am."

The thick head of his cock lines up with my entrance, and he grabs my ass cheeks and spreads them apart. It doesn't feel as warm as I expect, but then I remember that condom and a different kind of heat spreads through my chest. He came in here with that speech and those uncertain eyes and this kernel of foil-wrapped hope tucked away in his pocket.

When Fraser pushes inside me, it's too late. He's already lodged deep in my chest. And the steady rock of his hips once I've caught my breath, the delicious slick slide of him in and out of me… it's everything. It's the first hit of what will surely be a lifetime addiction, and god, is it the library making this so hot? Or is it *him*? Something tells me it's the man, with his rough hands and filthy words; the way he treasures and manhandles in one go. I thrust back against him, giving as good as I get, and gradually he swells larger and larger inside me.

"Raine," he chokes out. "Fuck. You feel magic." He smacks my ass again, harder this time, the sound cracking off my bare cheek. The hot sting, the sudden noise, the filthiness of it—it does something to me. Snaps the last thread of my control. I let out a low moan, tilting my hips so that he hits me *right there*, and when his fingers reach around and pinch my clit—I'm gone.

It's like falling. Toppling into an abyss, the wind rushing past my cheeks, and it goes on and on and on. Fraser stiffens inside me, his groan guttural, and his grip on my hip is tight enough to bruise.

Yes.

The feeling fills me to the brim. *Yes* to Fraser. *Yes* to these sensations. Just... *yes.*

"Good lord." Fraser recovers first, staggering to lean against the stacks and checking me over. I blow the sweaty strands of hair out of my face and level him a look, my cheek resting on the shelf.

"Don't give him all the credit."

He smirks, the corner of his mouth twitching up, and heat flares in my core again. I'm just about to reach for him, to pat him down for another condom, when the doors clatter open on the other side of the room. Hushed voices echo across the stacks—two students comparing notes for an exam. We yank our clothes back into place, breathless and laughing, then tiptoe through the shelves to the fire exit.

We thunder down the stairwell and out into the quad, hands

gripped tight. I'll make up the shift another day. Besides—it's nearly summer.

14

Epilogue

S he crosses the stage, her steps sure in those vicious heels, and accepts her diploma with a smile. It's no goofy grin—this is Raine after all, and she saves those unrestrained shows of emotion for those she loves. Lucy and Keeley and I. Maybe Beckett and Gideon on a good day. Raine turns and pauses for the photographer, supremely unruffled by the applause, then crosses the last distance to the other side of the stage.

I watch her, eagle-eyed. She may be unflappably confident, but I woke up in a cold sweat after dreaming she fell. But no, she nails it. The same way she nails everything; the same way she's graduating with honors. Her parents and little brother whoop from a few rows over, and I swallow, mouth suddenly dry.

Raine is not the only one facing a milestone today. She's graduating college. Finally being recognized for her intelligence and skill. And I'm meeting her rather loud parents.

God. I'd only do this for her.

She settles into her seat beside the stage, clapping calmly for the other graduates. Her black robes swamp her figure, but even here, even with her family nearby, I can't help but remember last night.

Vividly.

It was particularly energetic. Raine wanted to wrestle. Since our first adventure in the library, she's resumed her research into her own sexuality with incredible commitment.

And me? I'm the luckiest research assistant on earth. I'm more than happy to oblige.

The speeches take a small eternity. These functions always do. Graham drones on especially long, his eyes narrowing when he catches sight of me in the audience. I grin and wave, because what is he going to do? I don't work for the college anymore. And my new guidance counselor job with disadvantaged kids—it's somehow way less depressing than all my time here. He can take his grim little office and stuff it.

Raine drifts over as soon as the ceremony is over. Nearby, Keeley bounces up to Beckett, and Gideon and Lucy sway, already clasped together. Raine is too serene for that. For now, anyway. The second I get her alone, I'll work her into a wildcat.

"Have fun?" she asks, amusement tugging at her mouth.

"No," I tell her sadly. "I died of boredom at least three times."

She snorts, taking my hand and cringing as her parents call to her, her little brother jumping and waving.

"Are you sure?" she asks doubtfully, watching her family approach. Her mom's eyes drop to our clasped hands and brighten.

"Shut up." I squeeze her fingers. "I'm sure."

THE END

Thanks for reading After Class! I hope it gave you all the best student/professor feelings. & If you enjoyed it, please consider leaving a review!

For more steamy New Adult romance, be sure to check out Roomies. *He's her brother's best friend. He hates her guts. And now he's her roommate.* Read on for a sneak peek...

And for new releases, sales, and bonus content, be sure to sign up for my newsletter!

Kayla xx

Teaser: Roomies

I tug Theo's refrigerator open, wincing as the door groans on its hinges. I've only been in this apartment for five days, and I'm already getting a twitch. Every appliance, every surface, every piece of furniture—it's all worth more than I could possibly afford. When Theo sent me a spare key and a note offering me somewhere to crash, I can guarantee that he never dreamed I'd take him up on it. He knows I'm never comfortable in his place; that I'm too paranoid that I might damage something and not be able to pay.

Well, *surprise, Theo.* A place to live rent free for a few months while I save up for my own tattoo parlor—it's too good to turn down.

Especially since I emptied out my savings for my neighbor's son's medical bills.

Jesus. I can never tell Theo about that. He'd laugh so hard he cried, then insist on refilling my bank account. Easy as watering a house plant, never mind that I scraped and sweated for every last penny of those savings.

No. It's not going to happen. I made that choice and I stand by it. If I can undo it, easy as that, it doesn't *mean* anything. The rent-free apartment, though...

Yeah, I'll take him up on this. And with any luck, knowing Theo with his scattered world tours, I'll be long gone before he steps back on American soil. He never needs to know that it came to this. That I was desperate.

"Motherfucker." I shake out my hand, hissing, after catching my thumb in a cupboard drawer. For some reason, in this new, fancy environment, it's like I've never made a goddamn sandwich. Every chance I get to smack my elbow or nearly drop a mug—I take it. I'd figure it was some kind of self-sabotage, like I'm somehow trying to get caught out here, but it's always been like this with the Lanes.

Theo. And his little sister Florence. In their glossy, dazzling mansion full of sharp edges and stilted silences.

I can't count how many glass paned French doors I accidentally smudged over the years. How many ornamental flower beds I nearly trampled throwing a ball around with Theo after school. He never even registered the damage, so used to the staff members cleaning up behind him, but *I* noticed.

Jeez. I couldn't erase those moments from my brain.

This, at least, is Theo's place. His parents might pay the bills, but there are no staff members here. Only a cleaning lady that stops by every week, and I already told her to keep her wages and take the days off. That I'll let her know when I'm gone and she needs to come back again. She clucked and fussed over me for that, dusting my shoulders like I'm something else to clean, but she took me up on it.

Smart lady.

I carry my plate and mug through to the open plan living room, careful not to bump into anything. Theo's place is a typical bachelor pad—all sleek lines and stainless steel; monochrome paintings and a glass coffee table. It's soulless, but to Theo's credit, the first day he moved in, he had the rigid black leather sofa switched out for a bright teal fabric one which eats anyone who dares to sit on it.

I love that sofa. Half the nights here, I've fallen asleep on it.

The best part is the view. From the sofa, you can stare at the giant TV screen on the wall, sure. *Or,* you can gaze out at the balcony overlooking the city rooftops, the potted ivy climbing the balcony railings.

That ivy has Florence written all over it. It's understated beauty, an injection of character, and Theo probably hasn't noticed potted plants are a thing. He's charming, but oblivious. He definitely hadn't watered any of the ones here before I arrived.

So she brought it. I'm certain. I sip my coffee, frowning at the delicate white and green leaves, wrapping sensuously around the iron railings.

Yeah. That's Florence, alright.

The key sliding into the lock turns my body to stone. For the space between heartbeats, I sit rigid and horrified, the mug lifted halfway to my lips like a paused cartoon. It's okay that I'm here—I was invited, damn it—and Theo is always happy to see me. But *still,* I feel caught out. With my metaphorical pants down.

The door handle turns, the soft creak echoing through the apartment, and I jolt back to life. I put my mug down too hard, a dribble of coffee sloshing over the rim and pooling around the coaster. My throat is tight as I launch to my feet, tugging on the hem of my black t-shirt. Trying to come up with something, *anything* to say that will sound casual. Non-committal. Like a friend who decided on a whim to accept the invitation to crash, not a softhearted idiot who emptied out his savings for his neighbor.

Theo can't know. No one can know.

I have to take care of this myself.

The door swings open, and there's a thump. A muttered curse. And now my heart is twisting for a different reason, because I *know* that soft voice. Those careful, padding steps. Florence Lane moves through the world like she wishes she were a ghost. No noise, no space taken up.

When I was younger, it weighed on my chest. I wanted to make it better for her. And when I got older, when everything between us shifted and turned cold, it pissed me off. This girl was born to every privilege available, and she's still fragile? Really?

But the Florence who drags a straining duffel bag into the living room is not *fragile.* She's not careful and quiet. She kicks the door shut with her heel, cursing roundly with words that I didn't think she knew, and tosses the bag onto the floorboards with a bang. When she sees me, she jumps, her palm splaying over her chest, but she doesn't cringe away. Doesn't back down like she used to.

"Adrian." Her voice is flat. Amused, somehow, like she's in on some cosmic joke that I'm not. "Of course you're here. Why wouldn't you be?"

I shift my weight. Shove my hands into my pockets.

"Florence. Theo's not here." My eyes snag on her duffel bag again. That's not the bag of someone dropping around for a quick coffee with her brother.

She rolls her eyes, marching straight past me into the kitchen. Florence bustles around like someone who knows every inch of this place by heart, the process of making coffee a well-choreographed routine. She pulls a mug out of the dishwasher. Gets the right cupboard for coffee on the first try. Bumps the cutlery drawer shut with her hip.

"What are you doing here?" I try again, even though I have a sinking feeling that I already know. Florence shrugs, avoiding my gaze as she stirs her coffee briskly, flecks of liquid landing on the counter.

"Crashing. Theo sent me a key. You know how it is. Sometimes it's good to get away."

Lie. That's not the half of it. She won't even look at me, and besides—if that were all this is, she'd have turned around and left the second she saw me. Florence Lane cannot bear two minutes in my presence.

"Bullshit." Huh. Not my smoothest moment. But she's ruffled me; thrown me off kilter. "Theo already said I could stay. I've been here for a week already, Lane."

"And?" She smacks the spoon down on the counter. Turns to face me, cocking her hip.

I take her in. I can't help it. I've always been a sucker for Florence Lane's curves. The girl looks like she belongs in a sculptor's workshop. But her next words jolt me out of my reverie.

"This is *my* brother's place. Blood runs thicker than water, Griffith."

Low blow. Low fucking blow. And it only dawns on her after she's said it—how careless she's been. Why she shouldn't say shit like that to an ex-foster kid.

"Adrian—" she begins, but I cut her off. I don't even want to acknowledge it.

"The mansion not luxe enough for you? You can't stay in one of your family properties?" I tilt my head, smiling nastily. "Did they finally tuck you here out of sight?"

She sucks in a sharp breath, pain and anger flickering behind her eyes. I've hit a nerve without even trying, and I file that away for future reference. I need all the ammo I can get when it comes to this girl.

"I'm staying." Her voice is hoarse. She swipes up her mug, holding it tight enough that her knuckles turn white, but she doesn't take a sip. She just stares at me, chin raised in challenge. *"You've* got your own place. You've bragged about your independence enough. Why don't you scuttle back to it?"

Because I gave up my apartment the second I got your brother's offer.

Because this place is my last chance to get my life back on track.

I shrug, face blank. "I like it here. Getting a little taste of luxury." Why won't she drink her damn coffee? I'm getting a dry mouth just watching it hovering by her full lips. "Guess you'll have to learn to share. It'll be good for you. Character building."

She chokes out a laugh, but there's no humor to it. "We can't both stay here. I don't want to spend ten minutes with you."

"Off you go, then." I nod at the door. "Don't forget your bag."

"Adrian." She says my name low. It's a plea. "Stop messing with me and leave."

That's what am I to her. What I've always been. A curiosity at first, a fascination, then eventually a non stop pain in her ass. I don't have to try. I just have to *exist.* And she's always been able to dismiss me like one of her family's staff.

Not here. Not now. I have just as much right to be here. The damn key is digging into my thigh through my jeans pocket. If Theo offered the place to both of us, that's on him. He probably thought neither of us would go for it, but here we are.

And I'm not leaving. Not this time.

"Wipe that up when you're done." I nod at the flecks of coffee on the counter. "I sent the cleaning lady away."

"You—"

I don't hear what she calls me. I wheel around and stride across the apartment to the balcony, to the fresh summer breeze and the sunlit rooftops and the goddamn ivy fluttering in the wind.

* * *

It comes to me all at once. A flash of divine inspiration, as I'm eating my long abandoned sandwich hours later. I'm sitting on the balcony at the wrought iron table, telling myself that I'm not hiding from her. I'm just enjoying the view.

Every time I risk venturing back inside, she's still there. Spreading out. Pulling things out of her duffel. Making herself comfortable.

"Shit." I tear off a chunk of crust, chewing angrily. I'm not hungry. My stomach has been churning queasily since she crashed through that door, but I've always hated wasting food. "*Shit.*"

The thing about Florence is that's she's surprisingly stubborn. God knows she doesn't stand up for herself—apart from with me, apparently—but the girl nurses her grudges like she cultivates her house plants. She tends to them. Fusses over them. Coaxes them to grow up big and strong.

Hinting won't make her leave. Not even stating it outright. She won't go, not while she's determined to stick it out. Not while this apartment is a good place to be.

I get it. Her parents are kind of insane, in that unhinged, rich people way. I wouldn't last a week in that mansion. But the Lanes are loaded, and I've seen the family credit cards lining Florence's wallet first hand. She could go anywhere. A hotel, a spa, another country.

She could pull a Theo and disappear off around the world.
So—I can't change her mind. But I *can* change the context.
I can make this apartment hell, too.

* * *

Check Roomies out here.
    Brother's best friend.
    Enemies to lovers.
    Curvy heroine meets the tattooed hunk.
    What's not to love?

About the Author

Kayla Wren is a British author who writes steamy New Adult romance. She loves Reverse Harem, Enemies-to-Lovers, and Forbidden Love tropes.

Kayla writes prickly men with hearts of gold, secretly-sexy geeks, and—best of all—she's ALWAYS had a thing for the villains.

You can connect with me on:
- https://www.kaylawrenauthor.com
- https://www.bookbub.com/authors/kayla-wren
- https://www.amazon.com/~/e/B08CL281V1

Subscribe to my newsletter:
- https://www.kaylawrenauthor.com/newsletter

Also by Kayla Wren

Year of the Harem Collection:
Lords of Summer
Autumn Tricksters
Knights of Winter
Spring Kings

Standalone titles:
The Naughty List
Roomies

www.ingramcontent.com/pod-product-compliance
Lightning Source LLC
Chambersburg PA
CBHW030548130626
46552CB00006B/2486